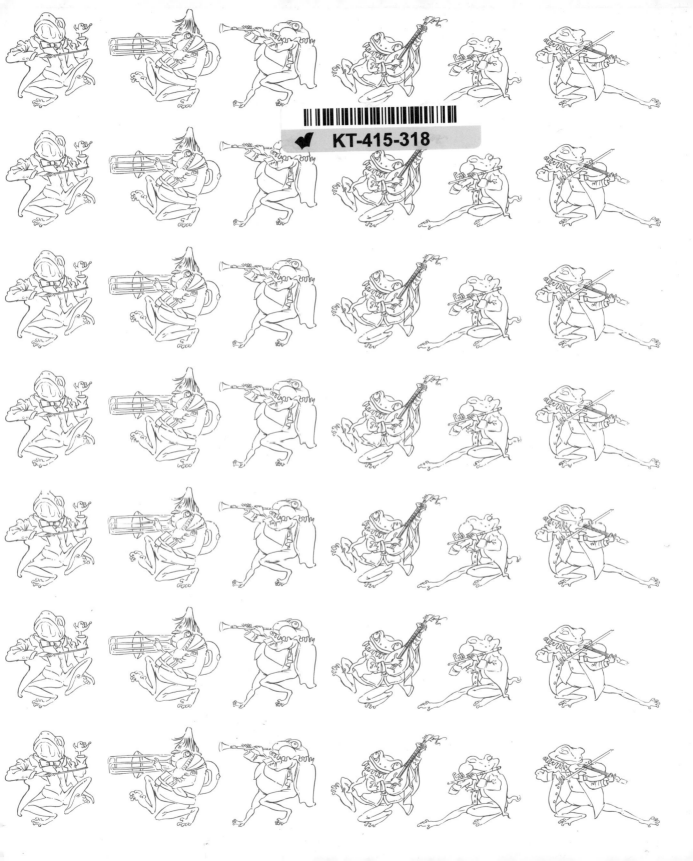

KT-415-318

To. REBECCA
HAPPY BIRTHDAY
LOVE NANNY. S.
1995.

# CLASSIC
# ANIMAL STORIES

# CLASSIC
# ANIMAL STORIES

Compiled by Lesley O'Mara

Illustrated by Angel Dominguez

Michael O'Mara Books Limited

First published in 1991 by
Michael O'Mara Books Ltd,
9 Lion Yard, Tremadoc Road, London SW4 7NQ

*Classic Animal Stories* copyright © 1991
by Michael O'Mara Books Ltd

Illustrations copyright © 1991 by Angel Dominguez

A CIP catalogue record for this book is available from the British Library

ISBN 1–85479–018–8

Editor: Catherine Taylor
Design: Mick Keates

Typeset by Florencetype Ltd, Kewstoke, Avon
Printed and bound in Hong Kong by Paramount Printing Group Ltd

For Mary Anne

# CONTENTS

# Contents

# LIST OF PLATES

8

# INTRODUCTION

THE ANIMAL STORIES in this collection are classics because they have been told and retold by successive generations, some for over two thousand years, others for only a century.

The oldest stories included here are the fables by Æsop. The word *fable* describes a particular type of animal story, one that comments on human conduct by depicting animals talking and reacting in the same way as people. Fables tend to have an obvious moral — which is often spelled out separately at the end so that no one misses the point! Very little is known about Æsop himself, but we can be fairly sure that he was a slave living on the Greek island of Samos in the sixth century B.C. and that he did compose many of the fables that bear his name.

More than two thousand years later, in seventeenth-century France, the writer Jean de La Fontaine included many of Æsop's tales in his own book of fables and became the other great name associated with this kind of animal story. La Fontaine gathered fables from many sources and also wrote some of his own.

Both Æsop's fables and those of La Fontaine were written down at the time they were composed, but many of the other stories in this book existed for many years before they were recorded. These are folk tales, which may have originated with one particular storyteller but over the centuries were adapted and changed as each generation told them to the next. Folk tales are less moralistic than fables, but they frequently depict the smaller, weaker animals getting the better of the more powerful ones, and in both fables and folk tales the animals speak, think and act like human beings. The writers with whom many of these tales are associated were merely the first people to write them down and publish them, rather than the original storytellers. The Brer Rabbit stories, for instance, were recorded in the 1870s by an American journalist named Joel Chandler Harris, who remembered the animal legends told by slaves on the Georgia plantation where he grew up and put them into the mouth of the fictional character Uncle Remus.

In the same way, the Grimm Brothers were not the original authors of the stories which bear their name – they collected their fairy tales from friends and acquaintances in early nineteenth-century Germany. Although their fairy tales have become classics of children's literature, the brothers themselves always regarded their work in a scholarly way, as material for the study of the history of German literature, and their first books were not designed to be attractive to children. Their contributors included the old nurse of the family next door and an elderly soldier who told stories in exchange for gifts of old trousers.

"The Three Goats Called Hurricane," which appears in this book, is a Scandinavian folk tale that was written down by two Norwegians – Peter Asbjørnsen and Jorgen Moe – in the last century. The stories they collected are often similar to folk tales that exist elsewhere in Europe, but they contain a distinctive Norse element. The troll appearing in "The Three Goats Called Hurricane" is a character from ancient Norse myths who has been absorbed into the folk tales.

Other classic animal stories are more recent. Rudyard Kipling's "Rikki-tikki-tavi" was first published in the 1890s, but it has earned its place in this collection by its timeless appeal, which has made it popular with each new generation of children.

Many folk tales and fables were first translated into English or transcribed many years ago, and so their language is dated and obscure. Joel Chandler Harris's Brer Rabbit stories in particular are full of local dialect that is not easily understood today. For this reason, when necessary the classic stories in this volume have been newly retold, in the tradition of folk tales, to make them more accessible to modern children.

# The Wicked Lord Chamberlain and the Kind Animals

Roman Folk Tale

IF YOU had been living in Rome about two thousand years ago and happened to be sitting in the woods outside the city, you might have witnessed a strange sight. You would have seen a very proud-looking man riding along on horseback, muttering to himself and suddenly disappearing down a pit.

This man was the Lord Chamberlain, an important official at the Emperor's court. His name was Marcus. He himself had ordered that pit, and many others, to be dug in the woods in order to catch wild beasts as they roamed about. Now Marcus himself had fallen into the pit, together with his horse. But they were not the only ones down there. Oh no! A monkey, a snake and a lion had already fallen in that same morning. Marcus roared out in terror, and luckily for him a poor woodcutter named Lucius happened to hear him and came to see what was happening. He stopped just on the brink of the pit and peeped warily down.

"Get me out quickly! Can't you see my life is in danger?" cried Marcus. "I'm rich and I will pay you anything you like."

"Your Excellency," said Lucius, "I'll help you if I can, but I shall need a long rope and I'll have to go into the city to get one. And that will take time. And during that time I shall not be able to chop any wood. And if I have no wood, I'll have none to sell. And if I don't sell any wood, my good wife and I will have no money to buy food."

"But if you get me out of this pit I'll make you very rich. You won't need to chop wood anymore," pleaded Marcus.

So Lucius went off into the city, got hold of some rope and returned quickly to the pit. He let the rope down and told Marcus to tie it round his waist. But before the Lord Chamberlain even had time to get hold of it, the lion sprang forward and used the rope to scramble up the side of the pit and escape. It ran off into the woods

and disappeared. Marcus now tried again, but this time the monkey jumped over Marcus's head, scrambled up and ran away among the trees. Marcus tried a third time. But now the snake twisted itself round the rope and Lucius, thinking it was Marcus tugging at the rope, pulled it up. When it got to the top, the snake slithered swiftly away and vanished into the undergrowth.

"I'm still here," bawled the Lord Chamberlain. "Let the rope down again and get me out of here quickly, I beg you."

At long last Lucius managed to pull him safely out. And then the two of them, Lucius and the Lord Chamberlain together, somehow succeeded in getting the rope round the horse's middle and pulling him out as well. But it was a hard struggle, I can tell you.

Then what do you think happened? As soon as he was safely at the top with his horse, Marcus rode back to the Emperor's court without so much as a word of thanks to Lucius.

When the woodcutter got home and told his wife of the day's happenings, she was, of course, disappointed that there was no firewood to sell but overjoyed at the news of the great reward her husband was going to receive from the Lord Chamberlain.

Next day Lucius set out for the court. He asked one of the flunkeys at the gates if he could see Marcus. The flunkey sent a messenger to find out, but he soon returned saying that Marcus knew nothing at all about Lucius; he had never heard of him and said that he must be telling a pack of lies. Furthermore he ordered Lucius to be given a good whipping and sent back where he came from. Lucius was so sore as a result of this that his poor wife had to come along to the court with their donkey to take Lucius back home and put him to bed.

After a few days, however, he went back to his woodcutting and firewood-selling. One morning he saw ten donkeys coming towards him, all laden with heavy packs. Behind them was a lion, and Lucius recognized it as the one he had pulled out of the pit. The lion nodded its head and waved its paw in the direction of Lucius's cottage. Lucius, slightly dazed by all this, led it to the cottage, where the lion, by further clever paw-signs, made it clear that the donkeys and the packs were now to belong to Lucius. Being a very honest man, Lucius led the donkeys round the village, inquiring whether anyone had lost them. He even put "LOST" notices in various shops. But nobody came to reclaim them. So Lucius opened the packs and to his great delight found they were all filled with gold. His wife shared his joy, of course, but she still made him go to work the following morning. In all the excitement, however, Lucius forgot to take his axe with him. He was just about to turn back when a monkey appeared in front of him – the very monkey Lucius had helped out of the pit. Using its teeth and claws it began to break good, solid pieces of wood from the trees and went on doing so until dusk, so that Lucius, even without his axe, had a plentiful supply of firewood to take back home.

And what do you think happened the next day? Well, of course, he met the snake he had rescued from the pit. It came slithering towards him with a colored stone in its mouth, dropped it at Lucius's feet and then vanished. It was a most beautiful stone, glittering and gleaming and sparkling with the brightest tints and hues. Lucius took the stone to a man who knew all about such matters. "Ah," he said in great amazement, holding it up to the light, "this stone will bring the greatest good luck to its owner. I am prepared to offer you any sum of money you care to ask for it." But Lucius, sensible man that he was, refused this tempting offer.

The news of the precious stone soon reached the court, and Lucius was summoned to appear before the Emperor. "That stone," said the

latter, "I *must* have. I will pay you whatever you ask. But if you are not prepared to sell it to me, your Emperor, then you must leave my kingdom and the lands which I rule for ever and ever."

Poor Lucius was left with no choice, so he handed the stone over to the royal hands and received five great sacks of gold in return.

Just as he was leaving the Emperor's presence, he heard the Imperial voice call out to him: "Come back, my good fellow, and tell me how a poor woodcutter like yourself came into the possession of so rare a stone."

"Well, Your Imperial Majesty, it was like this . . ." and Lucius told the whole story from beginning to end.

The Emperor listened with ever-increasing anger and amazement and by the end he was almost trembling with fury. He rose to his feet and called out: "Let the Lord Chamberlain be brought before me immediately."

When Marcus arrived and saw Lucius standing in front of the Emperor, who was pale with rage, his knees began to knock together in fear and trembling.

"Is this good man's story true?" demanded the Emperor. "Yes or no? Ah, I can see from your manner that the answer is yes and that you are indeed guilty of utterly shameful and disgraceful conduct, unworthy of a servant at my court. You are not fit to live."

But Lucius went down on his knees before the Emperor and pleaded for the cruel Lord Chamberlain's life. The Emperor was deeply moved by such generosity. "You owe your life to this humble woodcutter," he said to Marcus. "My order now is that you be banished from my kingdom for ever."

As for Lucius, he was given a post as Chief Guardian of the Imperial Forests and he lived happily with his wife to enjoy his wealth and position for many a long year.

# The Wolf
# and the
# Seven Little
# Kids

The Brothers Grimm

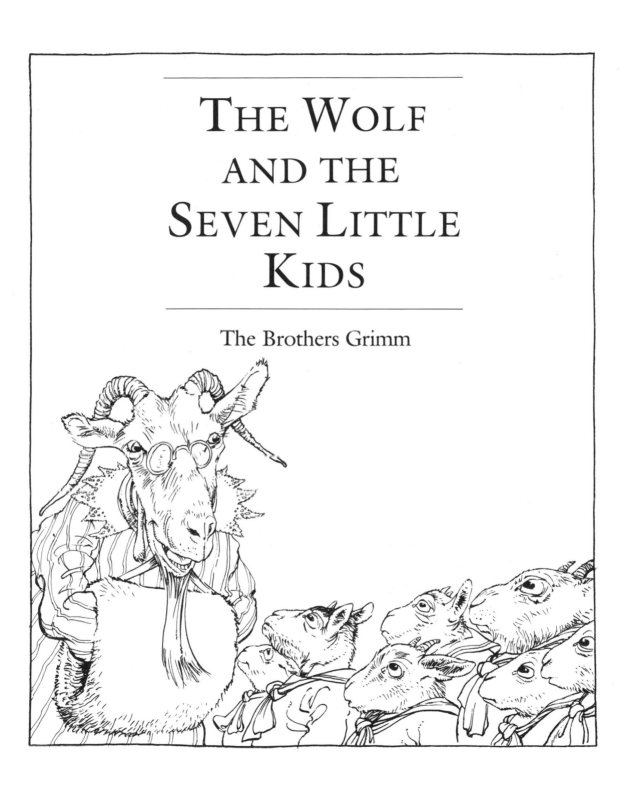

THERE WAS once an old mother goat who had seven kids. They all lived in a little house on the edge of a big, dark forest. One day, the mother goat had to go into the forest to collect food. Before she left, she called her seven kids to her and said: "Now, children, promise me that while I am away you will lock the door and be on your guard against the wicked wolf. If you see him, don't let him in, because he would certainly eat you all up. He might be dressed up, but you can recognize him by his gruff voice and his black paws."

"Yes, Mother," the kids replied, "we promise to be very careful." So the mother goat trotted cheerfully away into the forest, and the kids locked the door.

Some time later there was a knock at the door, and the kids heard a voice calling: "Open the door, children, it is I, your mother. I have brought back a present for each of you."

But the kids heard that the voice was gruff, and not the gentle voice of their mother, and so they called: "No, we will not let you in! You do not have a soft voice like our mother's, you have a gruff voice. You are the wolf!"

So the cunning wolf went to a shop and bought a stick of chalk and swallowed it to make his voice soft. Then back he went to the little house by the forest.

"Open the door, children," he called in his new soft voice. "It is your mother. I have brought back a present for each of you."

Now the kids heard the soft voice, but in his eagerness to get into the house the wolf had put his big black paws onto the window ledge, and so the kids cried out: "No, we will not let you in! Our mother has beautiful white feet, but you have black feet. You are the wolf!"

22

So the wolf ran back into the village. First, he went to the baker's shop.

"I have hurt my paw," he told the baker. "Please put some dough on it to soothe the pain."

When the baker had done this, the wolf ran off to the windmill, where the miller was grinding flour.

"Please put some flour on my paw," he asked.

At first the miller did not want to help. But the wolf said, "If you do not help me, I will gobble you all up." So the miller was afraid and did as he was asked.

The wolf ran back to the little house by the forest.

"Children, children, open the door!" he called again. "It is your mother. I have brought back a present for each of you."

The kids heard the soft voice but they could not see any paws, and they called out: "Let us see your paws so that we know you really are our mother."

So the wolf lifted up his paws, all white from the dough and the flour plastered on them. The kids thought that this time it really was their mother, and they unlocked the door.

The wolf rushed in. The kids screamed and tried to hide. One jumped into a drawer; the second squeezed under the bed; the third buried itself in the bedclothes; the fourth leapt into a cupboard; the fifth went into the oven; the sixth hid under a basin; and the littlest one slipped inside the grandfather clock. But the wolf found them and gobbled them all up – all except the youngest one hiding in the grandfather clock.

When the wolf had finished his meal, he felt very full and very sleepy. He wandered out of the house into a nearby meadow, lay down on some dry leaves, and promptly fell asleep.

When the mother goat came home from the forest, imagine her horror as she saw the door open, the furniture strewn around the house and the little kids all gone. She started calling them by name, but nobody answered until she called out the name of the youngest little kid, who was still hiding in the grandfather clock. She quickly pulled him out, and then they wept together as he told her what had happened to all his little brothers and sisters.

In her distress, she wandered out of the house with the little kid trotting beside her and soon found herself in the meadow where the wolf was sleeping. She looked carefully at him, and saw that there were six lumps in his big fat stomach, and that they seemed to be moving and struggling.

"How extraordinary!" she said. "Is it possible that my little kids are still alive?"

Quickly, she sent the youngest kid back to the house for scissors, needle and thread, and then she set to work cutting a hole in the wolf's stomach. Almost as soon as she had cut the first hole, a little kid popped out and with each hole she cut another of her children appeared, until all six of them were free, and jumping for joy around her. They had not come to any harm, for in his greed, the wolf had eaten them all whole!

"Quick," cried the mother goat, "fetch me some big stones so that I can fill up this wicked wolf's stomach."

So the little kids each fetched a big stone, and the mother goat put them into the wolf's stomach and sewed it up again so gently that the wolf felt nothing at all.

When the wolf awoke, he was very thirsty and set out to drink from the deep pool in the forest. The mother goat and the seven little kids followed behind him at a distance. As he walked along, the stones in

his stomach rattled and banged against each other, and made it difficult for him to walk. "What is the matter with me?" he thought to himself. "I thought I had eaten six tender young kids, but I feel as if I were full of stones."

When at last the wolf came to the pool, the mother goat gave a signal and all the goats got behind him and pushed and pushed until they had pushed him right into the water, where he sank straight to the bottom and drowned.

Then the little kids and their mother danced for joy. They would never have to be afraid of the wicked wolf again.

# Bertrand
# and
# Ratto

La Fontaine

H OW CLEVER I am!" said Bertrand the monkey to himself. And indeed he was. He was much cleverer than Ratto, the cat who lived in the same house.

Bertrand was not just clever and cunning. He was a thief too. And he often managed to get others to do his work for him.

Ratto the cat wasn't at all clever. He was lazy. He couldn't be bothered to hunt mice. Instead, he ate their cheese.

One day, Bertrand and Ratto sat by the fire where the servant girl had put chestnuts to roast.

"Ah!" Bertrand sniffed. "How good these chestnuts smell! I do wish I could have some. But my little paws could never pull the chestnuts from the fire. Oh dear!" And he sighed, watching the cat out of the corner of his eye.

"How I wish I was clever, like you!" he said to Ratto. "Quick and clever, that's what you are. I'm sure you could pull chestnuts out of the fire."

Ratto said, "Well, I could try."

"If Bertrand thinks I'm clever," he said to himself, "well then, I must be." Because Bertrand, everyone knew, was very clever indeed.

Ratto put out his paw, scratched the ashes and pulled two chestnuts from the fire.

"Well done!" Bertrand stretched out his paw and grabbed the chestnuts. "Ah," he said, "they're delicious. You should try them. Oh, but there aren't any left! Do you think you could pull any more from the fire? You really must have a taste of them."

Again Ratto pulled the chestnuts from the fire. Quickly the monkey snatched the chestnuts. "These are – mmmm – delicious. Oh," he said in dismay, "you've singed your paws. Do be careful this time."

Again, the cat pulled the chestnuts from the fire and again the

monkey snatched them up.

Just at that moment, a servant girl came into the kitchen. "What are you doing?" she said. "You bad Bertrand – and bad Ratto too!" She chased the pair of them into the yard.

"I didn't get any chestnuts at all," said the cat. "And look at my paws! They're all singed from the fire!"

"Oh dear, what a shame!" said the monkey. "Have I really eaten all the chestnuts?"

Ratto was angry and wouldn't speak to his friend the monkey. But Bertrand the monkey didn't care, did he? After all, he had had the chestnuts.

The moral of this story is that princes often do the work of kings. The princes are the ones who get their fingers burned, but the kings get the reward.

# Farmer Giles's Goats

## British Folk Tale

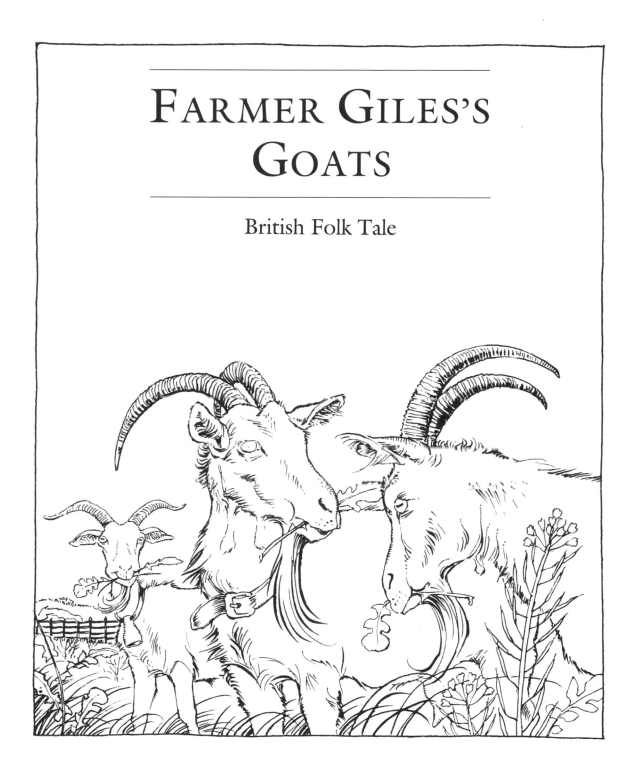

FARMER GILES had two fields. In one he grew some very nice turnips and in the other he kept his three goats – and very mischievous little goats they were.

One day the naughty goats ran out of their shed and into the turnip-field. Farmer Giles was very cross, but as he was too busy to see to the matter himself he sent his little boy. "Just run into the turnip-field, son," he said, "and drive those three naughty goats out at once."

Off ran the little boy to try and chase the goats out of the field. "Shoo, shoo, out you get, you naughty goats," he cried, but they took not the slightest notice. The little boy was soon gasping for breath and went and sat down by the gate and cried.

Soon a horse came along. "Why are you crying, boy?" asked the horse.

"Because I can't drive the goats out of my father's turnip-field," cried the lad.

"Is that all?" asked the horse. "I'll soon settle that for you." And he galloped into the turnip-field crying, "Out, out, you naughty goats," chasing them for all he was worth. But the goats simply ran away to the opposite end of the field. The horse was soon out of breath and went and sat down beside young Giles and, like him, began to cry. So now there were two of them boo-hooing; and the naughty goats carried on eating Farmer Giles's turnips.

Soon a cow came along. "Why are you two crying, may I be so bold to ask?" asked the cow.

"Because we can't drive Farmer Giles's goats out of his turnip-field," they howled.

"Don't worry, my friends, I'll soon see to that," said the cow, and she lumbered out into the field.

"Moo, moo, out you get, you naughty goats," she cried. But the goats ran much too fast for her and she was soon out of breath and gave up the chase. She, too, came panting over to young Giles and the horse and sat down and began to cry. So now there were three of them boo-hooing and boo-hooing. And the goats went on enjoying the turnips.

Next came a pig.

"And why, may I ask, are you lot crying your eyes out?" he queried.

"Because we can't drive the goats out of Farmer Giles's turnip-field," they wailed.

"Oho," said the pig. "I'll soon put that right." And off he trotted.

"Umph, grunt, humph, grunt, you naughty goats. Get out of this field this very minute, d'you hear!" he squealed.

But the goats didn't pay much attention to him. They ran to the opposite corner of the field and soon the pig, gasping for breath, gave up and came and sat down by young Giles, the horse and the cow. And now there were four of them, all boo-hooing their hearts out. The naughty goats, of course, just went on eating the farmer's turnips.

After a while a bee came buzzing along.

"What's the matter with you four, then?" he asked. "I could hear you crying from miles away."

"It's because we can't drive the goats out of Farmer Giles's turnip-field," they moaned.

"Not to worry," buzzed the bee, "I'll have them out in a jiffy."

The four of them stopped crying and stared in amazement at the bee.

"You could never do that," they said, "you're far too small." And they all burst out laughing.

"Just you wait," said the bee breezily, and off he flew into the

turnip-field. He came down low above the goats, soaring above their heads and buzzing away for all he was worth.

"Bzzzz! Bzzzz! Bzzzz!" he went. "If you goats don't clear out of this turnip-field this very minute, I shall fly down and sting the lot of you."

At this the three naughty goats galloped off as fast as their legs could carry them and never came back to the turnip-field again.

Young Giles, the horse, the cow and the pig were delighted. They thanked the bee and said, "My, what a clever little bee you are."

# THE GRATEFUL BEASTS

## The Brothers Grimm

ONCE UPON a time there lived a man who had lost nearly all his money.

"I have only a little left," he said to himself, "so I might as well travel and see the world and leave my troubles behind."

He hadn't gone very far when he came to a village, where the young people were all running about, shrieking and yelling excitedly.

"What's the matter?" he asked.

"Look!" said one, "we've caught a mouse – a dancing mouse! See how she jumps about when we tickle her!"

The man was very sorry for the poor mouse. "Let her go," he said. "Here's some money to pay for her."

So he took the mouse and set her free. In a moment she had scampered off and escaped down a hole.

In the next village, the man came across some children who were teasing a poor ass. They were making him jump about and stand on his hind legs like a human. The poor animal was exhausted and thirsty, but the children were all shouting and laughing and would not give him a moment's rest.

"Leave him alone," said the man. "Here, you can have this money, if you'll only let him go."

So the children shared the money between them, and the ass trotted off happily into the green fields.

It was evening when the man reached yet another village. Here he found that the young people had caught an old brown bear and were making him dance. The wretched animal could hardly grunt for weariness, but they would not stop tormenting him.

The man asked them to let the poor creature go free, and in exchange he gave them all the money he had left. As soon as the children let him go, the bear shambled off into the woods.

But now the man had no money left, not even a halfpenny to buy a crust for his supper.

He sat down by the roadside to think what to do. "I know," he said. "The King must have plenty of gold in his treasury that isn't any use to him. Perhaps I could borrow a little, just to buy food. And as soon as I have enough money again, I can pay it all back."

So he continued on his journey until he came to the palace of the King of that country. Stealthily, he crept into the King's treasury, and took three small pieces of gold out of one of the bags. But as he was leaving, the King's guards found him and, refusing to listen to a word he said, they dragged him before a judge.

The judge ordered the man to be shut up in a wooden chest and flung into the river. A few small holes were made in the lid of the chest to give him a little air, and a loaf of bread and a jug of water were placed inside.

The man sat miserably inside the chest as it bobbed along on the water and drifted down to the sea. He had floated only a few miles when he thought he heard a noise – it sounded like "nibble, nibble." In fact, it sounded very much like something gnawing at the lock.

Suddenly the lid of the chest sprang open – and there was a mouse. The very mouse he had set free! She had nibbled the lock in two in order to free the poor man.

And what's more, the ass and the bear were watching from the river bank, and as soon as they saw that the lid of the chest was open they swam out and helped to drag the box to the shore. How glad the man was to be safely on dry land!

The four friends were sitting on the bank, wondering what to do next, when a pure white stone shaped like an egg came floating past.

"Look!" cried the bear. "We're in luck! This is a magic stone. Whoever owns it can have anything he wishes for."

The man hurried down to the edge of the water and picked up the stone. "I wish," he said, "for a palace, a fine garden and a stable full of horses."

And there at once was a palace, a beautiful garden full of trees and fountains, and a magnificent stable with splendid horses. The man could hardly believe his eyes. He entered the palace, and there he lived in the greatest of luxury.

Not long after this a little group of merchants with their servants and mules and horses were passing that way.

"Look!" they said to each other. "Last time we were here, this place was just a desert. What can have happened?"

They were so curious that they went in through the palace gates and knocked at the great door. The man looked out at them through a little barred window.

The merchants questioned him: "Last time we came this way, there was nothing here but desert. Now there is a fine palace and beautiful gardens. How did it happen?"

When the man told them about the magic stone, they looked at each other in amazement and envy. "What a wonderful stone it must be," they said. The man invited them into the palace and showed them the stone, and immediately they began to bargain.

"Won't you sell it to us?" they begged him. "Look at all our beautiful things – you can have everything we've got if you'll only sell us the stone."

Now the merchants' goods were so fine and costly that the man completely forgot that as long as he had the stone he could have in an instant things a thousand times more beautiful than all the merchants'

wares. And because he forgot all this he agreed to the merchants' bargain.

No sooner did the stone leave his fingers than everything vanished from his sight – his fine palace and gardens, his splendid stables and horses – and he found himself sitting on the river bank, cooped up again in the chest, with only a jug of water and a loaf of bread.

But his friends – the mouse, the ass and the bear – hadn't forgotten him and they came at once to his rescue. The mouse did her best to loosen the lock on the chest, but this time she couldn't manage it.

"Friends," said the bear. "There is only one thing to do. We must find the stone." So off the three animals went.

They came to the palace where the merchants were now living and hid in a nearby grove of trees.

"Mouse," said the bear, "you're very small and quick. You creep in and peep through every keyhole and find out where the stone is kept."

The mouse did as she was told but she soon came back again. "I have bad news," she said. "I looked into the great hall and there I saw the stone. But it's hanging from the ceiling by a red silk string in front of a mirror. On either side of the stone there sits a huge cat with fiery flashing eyes, guarding it."

"Go back again," said the bear, "and wait until the master of the palace is asleep. Then nip his nose with your sharp teeth and pull his hair."

The mouse went back to the palace and crept this way and that until at last she came to the very best bedroom. There was a great fourposter bed with silk hangings. In the bed lay the chief of the merchants, sound asleep. The mouse crept up to him, nipped his nose with her sharp teeth and tugged at his hair.

Immediately he woke up, clutching his nose and shouting, "You're a

pair of useless good-for-nothing cats! You'd let the mice gnaw the nose off my face and pull the hair off my head and not move a whisker!"

And he leapt out of bed, rushed into the hall and drove the two cats with the flaming eyes out of the palace.

The next night, the mouse returned. She crept into the hall and, perching on her hind legs, nibbled and nibbled at the silk string on which hung the magic stone until it snapped and the stone fell on to the soft silk carpet beneath.

She nudged the stone with her nose until little by little she managed to move it. At last she reached the door through which she had entered the palace. She nibbled at the wood until she had made an opening wide enough to push the stone through. And there, waiting for her on the other side, was the ass.

To keep the stone safe, he put it into his mouth under his long tongue and off they went together to the river, where the bear was waiting.

The bear scrambled down into the water. "Put your forefeet on my shoulders," he told the ass, "and hold still."

The mouse sat in the bear's right ear, and the bear began swimming. But they hadn't gone very far before he started boasting.

"I'm a very fine swimmer," he said. "Don't you think so?"

The ass didn't say a thing. This made the bear very cross.

"Why don't you answer?" he said. "Weren't you taught to speak when you're spoken to?"

The ass opened his mouth to reply and the magic stone rolled out from under his tongue and sank to the bottom of the river.

"How could I speak?" he brayed. "I had the stone in my mouth. And now it's gone forever – and it's all your fault."

One morning he saw ten donkeys coming towards him, all laden with heavy packs
(*The Wicked Lord Chamberlain and the Kind Animals*)

He . . . lay down on some dry leaves, and promptly fell asleep
(*The Wolf and the Seven Little Kids*)

Ratto put out his paw, scratched the ashes and pulled two chestnuts from the fire
(*Bertrand and Ratto*)

. . . all boo-hooing their hearts out (*Farmer Giles's Goats*)

"Oh, be quiet," said the bear. "Let's go back to shore and think what to do."

So they talked things over and at last they went to the King of Frogs. They asked him to call together all his subjects, their wives and children, brothers and sisters, aunts and uncles, and all their relations and friends.

When they'd gathered together, the King of Frogs called out, "My people, there's an enemy on the way. But we'll be ready for him. Bring in all the stones you can find and we'll build a huge fortress."

The frogs were very alarmed but they set to work, bringing stones from the river and piling them into heaps. At last an old fat bull frog appeared, dragging behind him by its silk string – the magic stone!

The bear and his friends jumped for joy, and thanked the King of Frogs again and again for his kindness.

"The danger has passed now," said the King of Frogs to his people, "but if the enemy does appear, well, we're ready for him."

Then the three friends set off at once down the river. There was barely a moment to spare when they reached the chest. The poor man had eaten up every crumb of the loaf, and there was no water left in the jug. With almost his last breath, he wished himself back in the palace.

Then he wished again – and there were the merchants outside the gate with all their merchandise restored to them. They would never get inside the palace again.

The man and his three good animal friends lived happily together in the fine palace, with its beautiful gardens and splendid stables. Everything they could possibly want they had, for the magic stone granted their every wish.

# CHANTICLEER AND PERTELOTTE

## Chaucer

ONCE UPON a time there lived a poor old widow and her two daughters in a little cottage by the meadow.

She had a small farm with some pigs, a cow called Daisy, a sheep called Molly, seven fine-looking hens and a magnificent rooster called Chanticleer. He really was a grand-looking bird, with a comb as red as flaming fire, a coal-black beak and feathers glowing bright with many colors. How fine he looked as he strutted proud and upright in the farmyard.

No other rooster in the land could crow as loudly or as beautifully as Chanticleer, and the old widow and her two daughters were very proud of him.

One night Chanticleer had a strange dream and it worried him so much that he woke up his wife, Pertelotte, to tell her all about it.

"I've had a really nasty dream, my dear," he said. "I was walking up and down the yard when I saw a strange animal come racing towards me. It was a brownish-reddish color, but it had a kind of black fur above its eyes and its long bushy tail was jet-black too. Its eyes gleamed like coals of fire, and just as it was about to seize me in its jaws I woke up."

"Shame on you, husband," cried Pertelotte. "Fancy a great strong rooster like you being afraid of dreams. Dreams don't mean a thing." And she closed her eyes and went back to sleep again. Chanticleer felt a wee bit ashamed, but though he didn't bother Pertelotte anymore he feared secretly that his dream might come true.

The next morning Chanticleer was strutting proudly round the farmyard followed by Pertelotte and the six hens. But not very far away in a bed of cabbages, a big red fox lay in hiding, waiting to pounce upon Chanticleer. Chanticleer had strutted on ahead of the hens and suddenly he caught a glimpse of the fox's face. It reminded

him of the animal he had seen in his dream and he was just about to run away when the sly fox called out:

"Good morning, Sir Chanticleer, don't run away. I am your friend and I was the friend of your father before you. Whenever I hear your fine voice crowing in the morning I remember your father, who had a wonderful voice like yours. He often used to sing to me when I asked him to, for I did admire his voice. You could hear it for miles around, over hill and dale, just like yours. Won't you please sing for me, just this once? Just like your dear father did, with your eyes tightly closed, standing on your tiptoes and your neck stretched right out. Please sing for me, just this once, Sir Chanticleer."

You may well imagine Chanticleer was delighted to hear all these nice remarks about his voice, for he was secretly very proud of it and thought there was no other rooster to compare with him. So for the moment he forgot all about his bad dream and his fear of the fox, and he said:

"Yes, Mr. Fox, I will sing for you."

And so standing high upon his toes, and stretching his neck right out, and closing his eyes tight, and opening his coal-black beak, he began to sing with all his might: "Cock-a-doodle-doo!"

At that instant the sly fox leapt up, grabbed him by his neck, flung him over his back and raced off into the woods.

When Pertelotte saw that her beloved Chanticleer had disappeared, she started cackling at the top of her voice and running this way and that in great excitement. And all the other hens started to do likewise. And when the old widow and her two daughters heard all the noise in the farmyard they too came running out. And they all started running after Mr. Fox, whom they could see galloping off in the distance with Chanticleer flung over his back. Soon they were joined by the ducks and geese from the pond and all the bees from the beehives, and by Talbot and Shaggy, the two collie-dogs belonging to Farmer Giles, the next door neighbor, and by Farmer Giles himself. And his two farmhands, Jenkins and Humphrey, joined in the chase, shouting fearful cries and waving long sticks in the air.

And when Chanticleer saw all the great crowd that was chasing Mr. Fox, he took courage and said to Mr. Fox:

"I say, Mr. Fox, why don't you turn round and tell all those silly people not to be so stupid. Just turn round and tell them that you mean to eat me up no matter what *they* do or say. Tell them you'll soon be safe in your lair and that they'll never be able to catch you." When Mr. Fox heard this he said:

"How right you are, Sir Chanticleer, I shall certainly do so."

But the moment he opened his mouth the rooster jerked himself away and flew high up into the nearest tree.

And Mr. Fox, seeing that he had made a great mistake in opening his mouth, called out to Chanticleer:

"Come down, my friend. I'm sorry I scared you. I must have grabbed you too hard when I caught hold of you. Come down again, I won't hurt you this time."

But Chanticleer was not to be fooled again. And turning to Mr. Fox he said: "Oh no, Mr. Fox, you'll never get me again. You'll never catch me again with my eyes shut." And then he flew down and ran back to Pertelotte and the old widow. And everybody was very happy to have him back safe and sound once more.

# Tiger in the Forest, Anansi in the Web

### West Indian Folk Tale

FOR A time Anansi and Tiger were friends. Anansi liked to be with Tiger, who was strong, while Tiger was amused by the tricks that clever Anansi played on all the animals, using his wits to avoid doing any work, yet always managing to persuade Monkey or Hen, Dog or Puss to share their meals with him. When everyone was hard at work, Anansi watched from the shade of a tree, yet his bag of food was always full, and his wife and children had enough to eat.

In the hot season Anansi and Tiger went every day to the river for a swim. One day Tiger took with him a delicious stew that his wife had made, with large dumplings, thick gravy, and tender pieces of meat of the gibnut and accouri. This was Tiger's favorite dish and it was also a dish that Anansi could not resist. As the two friends strolled down to the river, Anansi kept his eyes on the large tin of stew. The smell made his mouth water so that he could hardly talk; and he began to think of ways of getting the stew for himself.

"Let's try a new place for our swim, Tiger," said Anansi; "up by the rocks where there is a deep hole, so deep that everybody calls it the Blue Hole."

"Very well," replied Tiger. "But do you think that you can swim there, Anansi? That is deep water."

"You swim so well that I won't worry," said Anansi. "If I get into trouble I know you will help me, Tiger, for we are good friends. We share everything."

"But I can't share my lunch with you today," replied Tiger. "This stew of accouri and gibnut is my favorite. My wife got the meat in the market and cooked it specially for me. You can smell how good it is, can't you, Anansi?"

"Yes, I can. Yes, I can. Yes, yes," said Anansi with that strange, soft lisp of his. He pronounced "s" like "sh," and spoke in a high-pitched voice. The smell of the stew was so tempting that he could not take his eyes off the tin.

At the Blue Hole, Anansi said, "Brother Tiger, you are a big man, you go in and try out the water first. I will come in after you."

Tiger replied, "Very well, Brother Anansi. I will put the tin of stew where no one can trouble it, on this stump of an old cotton tree. There I can keep my eyes on it. Then I will dive in. But you must come in when I call you. I am not going to leave you with that stew for long."

"You go first, and try out the depth of the water," said Anansi, "and I will follow."

Tiger dived in. Anansi shouted, "Try out the deep, deep parts, Tiger, where it looks blue-blue, yes, yes."

Tiger loved swimming and diving. He took a deep breath and dived, trying to reach the sandy bottom of the river, but the water was deeper than he expected. He came up to the surface, looked round quickly to make sure that his stew was safe, took a deep breath, and dived again. While Tiger was under the water, Anansi emptied the tin of stew on to a large green plantain leaf, put the tin back on the stump and sat in the shade where Tiger could not see him. There he quickly ate the stew, while Tiger dived and swam. At last Tiger called out:

"Come in, Anansi, come in." He could see the tin on the stump where he had left it. "Ah," he thought, "soon I will have my lunch." Then he shouted, "You are a lazy fellow, Anansi. I am coming to throw you into the water!"

Anansi was very frightened. What would Tiger do when he found that the tin was empty? He called out:

"No, Tiger, no; I am frightened. I don't want to be thrown into the water. I am going back home."

Anansi hurried to Big Monkey Town, which was only half a mile away. He said to Big Monkey, "Brother Monkey, I was down at the Blue Hole with Tiger and I heard them sing a song (he said "shing a shong") and this is how it went:

> *"This lunch-time I ate Tiger's stew,*
> *This lunch-time I ate Tiger's stew,*
> *This lunch-time I ate Tiger's stew*
> *But Tiger didn't know."*

Big Monkey shouted to Anansi, "What nonsense. Run away. Leave our town. We don't want to hear your silly song."

Anansi hurried on to Little Monkey Town nearby, where all the little monkeys lived, the small brown monkey, the marmoset, and the capuchin monkey. He said to them:

"Brer Monkey, I heard a sweet, sweet song down by the river, and this is what it said:

> *"This lunch-time I ate Tiger's stew,*
> *This lunch-time I ate Tiger's stew,*
> *This lunch-time I ate Tiger's stew*
> *But Tiger didn't know."*

"That's a good dance-tune," cried Capuchin Monkey, who loved nothing better than dancing, "a very good dance-tune indeed. Let's learn it."

All the little monkeys began to learn the song. They said to Anansi, "Sing it slowly, so we can get the tune right." Anansi sang the song

over and over again until the little monkeys had learnt it. Then they said:

"Anansi, we will have a big dance tonight, and you must come back to hear us sing this song."

That evening, when Anansi heard the little monkeys singing the song and dancing, he hurried off to Tiger, who was in a rage, questioning animal after animal about his lunch.

"Come with me, Tiger," said Anansi, "and you will find out what you want to know. Do you know what they are singing in Little Monkey Town? Listen."

The sound of singing and music came faintly on the night wind. Anansi began to pick up the words of the song as if they were new to him. "I can't get it all, Tiger, but it's something about eating Tiger's stew and Tiger didn't know."

Tiger and Anansi raced off to Little Monkey Town, Tiger bounding along with great strides so that Anansi could hardly keep up with him. Near the town, Anansi said:

"Hide in the bush, Tiger, for we must make sure first. Listen."

The little monkeys were playing and singing and dancing to the tune Anansi had taught them:

*"This lunch-time I ate Tiger's stew,*
*But Tiger didn't know."*

"Hear that, Tiger?" asked Anansi. "Didn't I tell you? Do you hear? Listen again. There it is – "

*"This lunch-time I ate Tiger's stew,*
*But Tiger didn't know."*

"But I know now," roared Tiger, breaking through the bush into Little Monkey Town, with Anansi behind him. He leaped through an open window into the middle of the dance-hall and cried:

"So you ate my stew, did you?"

"What are you talking about?" asked one of the little monkeys. "We learnt that song from Anansi."

Tiger was too enraged to listen. "I am going to teach you all a lesson," he shouted, his teeth flashing in the light.

Capuchin Monkey, the fastest runner of all, made for Big Monkey Town at full speed to ask for help, while Tiger and Anansi began to attack the little monkeys, who were scattering in fright. Soon a troop of big monkeys arrived. At the sight of them Tiger took to the bush. He lives there to this day. Anansi, frightened almost out of his wits, climbed up into the top of the house. He lives there safe in his web, hiding from the monkeys.

The frogs were very alarmed . . . (*The Grateful Beasts*)

. . . he began to sing with all his might: "Cock-a-doodle-doo!"
(*Chanticleer and Pertelotte*)

The sound of singing and music came faintly on the night wind
(*Tiger in the Forest, Anansi in the Web*)

"Who is that crossing my bridge?" boomed the troll
(*The Three Goats Called Hurricane*)

# THE THREE GOATS CALLED HURRICANE

Scandinavian Folk Tale

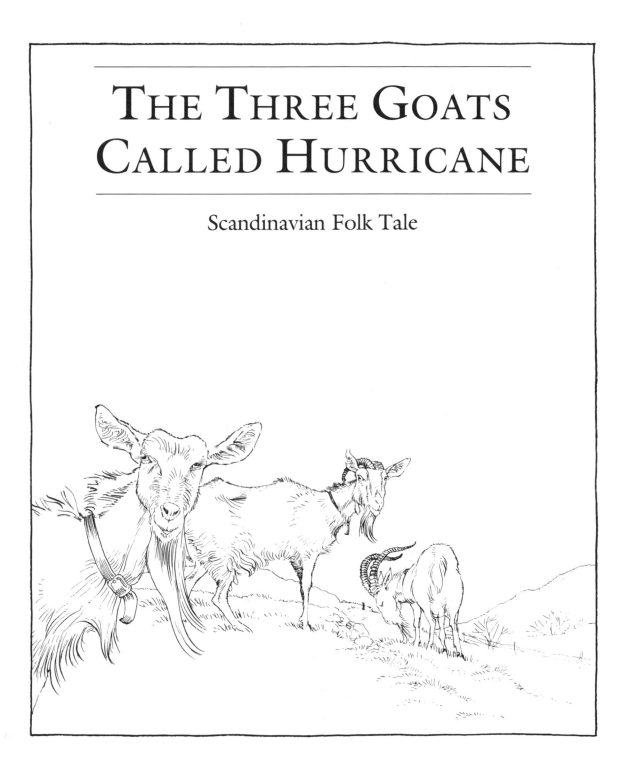

ONCE UPON a time there were three goats who lived together on a steep hillside and they were all called Hurricane. One day they decided to go to graze on the lush green grass that covered a nearby hillside. In order to get there, however, the goats had to cross a bridge over a deep river. Underneath this bridge lived a wicked troll, with eyes as big as saucers, and a nose as long as a broomstick.

Well, the first goat came along and started to trot clip-clop clip-clop over the bridge.

"Who is that crossing my bridge?" boomed the troll from underneath the bridge.

"It is I, the little goat Hurricane," replied the goat timidly, in his tiny high voice. "I am going to the hillside to graze."

"Oh, no you're not!" cried the troll. "I'm coming to gobble you up!"

"Oh, I shouldn't bother about me," replied the goat. "I am only very small. The other goat Hurricane will be crossing the bridge in a few moments, and he is much bigger than I am. Why don't you wait for him?" And so saying, he trotted off to the hillside.

Sure enough, a few minutes later, the second goat came trotting clip-clop clip-clop onto the bridge.

"Who is that crossing my bridge?" boomed the troll.

"It is I, the second goat Hurricane," replied the goat in his louder, deeper voice. "I am going to the hillside to graze."

"Oh, no you're not!" cried the troll. "I'm coming to gobble you up!"

"Oh, don't waste your time catching me," replied the goat. "I am really not very large. The big goat Hurricane will be coming past soon, and he is much bigger than I am. Why don't you wait for him?" And

he trotted away to the hillside.

And, just as he had said, a little while later, the big goat came thudding clomp clomp clomp onto the bridge.

"Who is that thudding across my bridge?" thundered the troll.

"It is I, the big goat Hurricane," replied the goat in his strong, deep voice.

"Aha!" cried the troll. "I have heard about you. I am coming to gobble you up!"

"Come and get me then!" replied the big goat Hurricane. "I have two strong horns on my head, and I can soon deal with a wicked brute like you!" And he lowered his head and butted the troll with his horns, and trampled on him with his feet, and finally pushed him off the bridge and down into the deep river below. Then he strode off up on to the hillside to join the other two goats.

And then they all ate and ate and ate until they could eat no more.

# THE COUNCIL HELD
# BY THE RATS

La Fontaine

**B**EWARE OF Rodiland!" The message went all round the kingdom of the rats. "Beware of Rodiland!" the rats told one another, and they shook with fear.

"Who is Rodiland?" asked a very young rat.

"He's never heard of Rodiland!" said an older rat, amazed.

"Oh, I wish *we* had never heard of Rodiland," said another.

"Tell me," said the young rat eagerly, "who is Rodiland?"

"You will know soon enough," said an older, wiser rat. "He is a cat, a very old cat, who catches rats. If you should see him, with his whiskers twitching and his eyes shining, then run – run for your life," he said solemnly.

"We are all afraid of Rodiland," said another, "but there is nothing we can do."

As time went on, Rodiland, the rat-catching cat, ate so many rats that only a few were left, some old, some middle-aged and the very young rat. By now, they were so terrified that they did not dare leave their homes to look for food.

One day, they peeped out from their holes in fear and trembling as Rodiland prowled out to meet his wife. "Miaow," they heard him call. "Miaow," his wife replied.

The sound struck terror into the hearts of the few rats who were left.

"Come," said the oldest, wisest rat, "we must have a meeting and decide what to do. If things go on like this, we shall starve, for we cannot leave our homes to find food for fear that Rodiland will catch us."

So the rats sat down together. At last, the oldest, wisest rat said, "I've got it! I have a splendid idea!"

They all turned to him. "Tell us your idea!"

"It is this," said their leader. "We get a bell and hang it around Rodiland's neck. Then the bell will ring whenever he comes near and we shall know to stay safely underground."

"Bravo!"

"A splendid idea!"

"That's the answer!"

The rats all applauded, and the oldest, wisest rat looked modest. After all, he was their leader, so he was bound to have the best ideas.

"Now," – he held up his paw – "we must decide which of us is to hang the bell around Rodiland's neck."

He paused. "I am your leader, so I must stay here to plan and decide things. It is not for me to bell the cat. Besides, I am much too old." He looked at the next oldest rat.

"Not I," said the second oldest. "I have a wife to look after."

"Are you afraid?" asked the leader scornfully.

"Yes," said the second oldest rat. "I am. It is a very dangerous job. It is a job for someone younger."

"Well, then," said the leader. "Who?" He looked at the next in line. "What about you?"

"Oh, no," said the next rat hastily. "I might not come back. Certainly it is the answer to all our problems, but no – it is a job for someone young and fit."

So it went on. All the rats said it was a splendid idea, but they didn't want to be the one to bell the cat.

At last the leader looked at the youngest rat. "It's a task for a very young rat," he said. "It's a great privilege to be asked to bell the cat. You will do a service to all ratdom. I wouldn't be surprised if you got a medal for it. Think of it – a beautiful silver medal to wear! How proud your mother would be!"

The youngest rat was just about to say "I'll do it!", thinking of the rewards and how proud his mother would be. But then it struck him. "How do I get the bell around Rodiland's neck?" he asked. "He would catch me and eat me before I had a chance." And it was suddenly clear to him that this would be a very dangerous task. "No, thank you," he said quickly. "It is much too difficult and dangerous a job."

"So no one will bell the cat," said the leader.

They all shuffled and looked at one another, and the meeting broke up. In the distance they could hear above ground Rodiland on the prowl. "Miaow! Miaow!"

And the moral of this story? There are usually lots of people to say what should be done. But it is not so easy to get someone to agree to undertake the task.

# RIKKI-TIKKI-TAVI

Rudyard Kipling

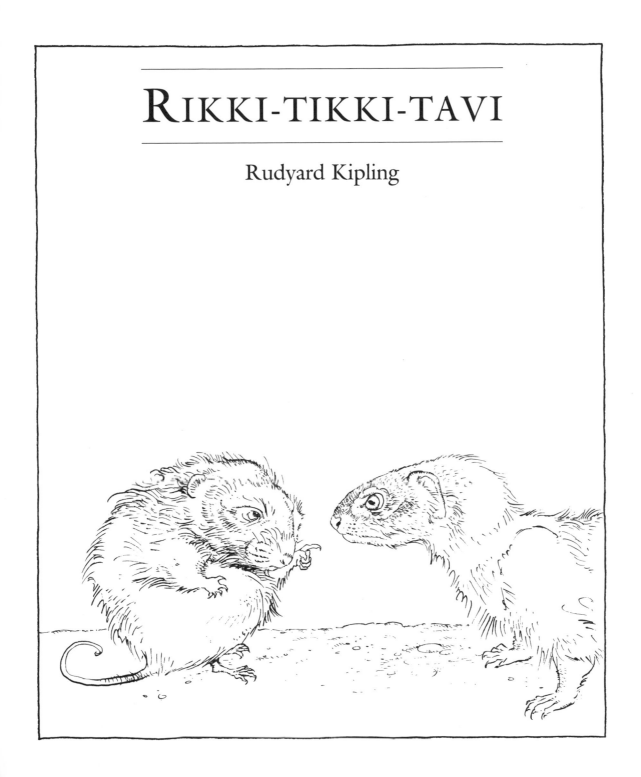

At the hole where he went in
Red-Eye called to Wrinkle-Skin.
Hear what little Red-Eye saith:
"Nag, come up and dance with death!"

Eye to eye and head to head,
(*Keep the measure, Nag.*)
This shall end when one is dead;
(*At thy pleasure, Nag.*)
Turn for turn and twist for twist —
(*Run and hide thee, Nag.*)
Hah! The hooded Death has missed!
(*Woe betide thee, Nag!*)

THIS IS the story of the great war that Rikki-tikki-tavi fought single-handed, through the bathrooms of the big bungalow in Segowlee cantonment. Darzee, the tailor-bird, helped him, and Chuchundra, the musk-rat, who never comes out into the middle of the floor, but always creeps round by the wall, gave him advice; but Rikki-tikki did the real fighting.

He was a mongoose, rather like a little cat in his fur and his tail, but quite like a weasel in his head and his habits. His eyes and the end of his restless nose were pink; he could scratch himself anywhere he pleased, with any leg, front or back, that he chose to use; he could fluff up his tail till it looked like a bottle-brush, and his war-cry, as he scuttled through the long grass, was: '*Rikk-tikk-tikki-tikki-tchk!*'

One day, a high summer flood washed him out of the burrow where he lived with his father and mother, and carried him, kicking and clucking, down a roadside ditch. He found a little wisp of grass floating there, and clung to it till he lost his senses. When he revived, he was lying in the hot sun on the middle of a garden path, very draggled indeed, and a small boy was saying: "Here's a dead mongoose. Let's have a funeral."

"No," said his mother; "let's take him in and dry him. Perhaps he isn't really dead."

They took him into the house, and a big man picked him up between his finger and thumb, and said he was not dead but half choked; so they wrapped him in cotton-wool, and warmed him, and he opened his eyes and sneezed.

"Now," said the big man (he was an Englishman who had just moved into the bungalow); "don't frighten him, and we'll see what he'll do."

It is the hardest thing in the world to frighten a mongoose, because he is eaten up from nose to tail with curiosity. The motto of all the mongoose family is "Run and find out"; and Rikki-tikki was a true mongoose. He looked at the cotton-wool, decided that it was not good to eat, ran all round the table, sat up and put his fur in order, scratched himself, and jumped on the little boy's shoulder.

"Don't be frightened, Teddy," said his father. "That's his way of making friends."

"Ouch! He's tickling under my chin," said Teddy.

Rikki-tikki looked down between the boy's collar and neck, snuffed at his ear, and climbed down to the floor, where he sat rubbing his nose.

"Good gracious," said Teddy's mother, "and that's a wild creature! I suppose he's so tame because we've been kind to him."

"All mongooses are like that," said her husband. "If Teddy doesn't pick him up by the tail, or try to put him in a cage, he'll run in and out of the house all day long. Let's give him something to eat."

They gave him a little piece of raw meat. Rikki-tikki liked it immensely, and when it was finished he went out into the veranda and sat in the sunshine and fluffed up his fur to make it dry to the roots. Then he felt better.

"There are more things to find out about in this house," he said to himself, "than all my family could find out in all their lives. I shall certainly stay and find out."

He spent all that day roaming over the house. He nearly drowned himself in the bath-tubs, put his nose into the ink on a writing-table, and burnt it on the end of the big man's cigar, for he climbed up in the big man's lap to see how writing was done. At nightfall he ran into Teddy's nursery to watch how kerosene-lamps were lighted, and when Teddy went to bed Rikki-tikki climbed up too; but he was a restless companion, because he had to get up and attend to every noise all through the night, and find out what made it. Teddy's mother and father came in, the last thing, to look at their boy, and Rikki-tikki was awake on the pillow. "I don't like that," said Teddy's mother; "he may bite the child." "He'll do no such thing," said the father. "Teddy's safer with that little beast than if he had a bloodhound to watch him. If a snake came into the nursery now – "

But Teddy's mother wouldn't think of anything so awful.

Early in the morning Rikki-tikki came to early breakfast in the veranda riding on Teddy's shoulder, and they gave him banana and some boiled egg; and he sat on all their laps one after the other, because every well-brought-up mongoose always hopes to be a house-mongoose some day and have rooms to run about in, and Rikki-tikki's mother (she used to live in the General's house at Segowlee) had carefully told Rikki what to do if ever he came across white men.

"I've got it! I have a splendid idea!" (*The Council Held by the Rats*)

"Indeed and truly, you've chosen a bad place to be lame in."
(*Rikki-tikki-tavi*)

. . . the tomtit called together the birds of the air and a very large army of hornets, gnats, bees, flies, and other insects (*The Tomtit and the Bear*)

"Well," said the fox, "I know a hundred clever tricks." (*The Cat and the Fox*)

Then Rikki-tikki went out into the garden to see what was to be seen. It was a large garden, only half-cultivated, with bushes as big as summer-houses of Marshal Niel roses, lime and orange trees, clumps of bamboos, and thickets of high grass. Rikki-tikki licked his lips. "This is a splendid hunting-ground," he said, and his tail grew bottle-brushy at the thought of it, and he scuttled up and down the garden snuffing here and there till he heard very sorrowful voices in a thornbush.

It was Darzee, the tailor-bird, and his wife. They had made a beautiful nest by pulling two big leaves together and stitching them up the edges with fibers, and had filled the hollow with cotton and downy fluff. The nest swayed to and fro, as they sat on the rim and cried.

"What is the matter?" asked Rikki-tikki.

"We are very miserable," said Darzee. "One of our babies fell out of the nest yesterday, and Nag ate him."

"H'm!" said Rikki-tikki, "that is very sad – but I am a stranger here. Who is Nag?"

Darzee and his wife only cowered down in the nest without answering, for from the thick grass at the foot of the bush there came a low hiss – a horrid cold sound that made Rikki-tikki jump back two clear feet. Then inch by inch out of the grass rose up the head and spread hood of Nag, the big black cobra, and he was five feet long from tongue to tail. When he had lifted one-third of himself clear of the ground, he stayed balancing to and fro exactly as a dandelion-tuft balances in the wind, and he looked at Rikki-tikki with the wicked snake's eyes that never change their expression, whatever the snake may be thinking of.

"Who is Nag?" said he. "*I* am Nag. The great god Brahm put his mark upon all our people when the first cobra spread his hood to keep

the sun off Brahm as he slept. Look, and be afraid!"

He spread out his hood more than ever, and Rikki-tikki saw the spectacle-mark on the back of it that looks exactly like the eye part of a hook-and-eye fastening. He was afraid for the minute; but it is impossible for a mongoose to stay frightened for any length of time, and though Rikki-tikki had never met a live cobra before, his mother had fed him on dead ones, and he knew that all a grown mongoose's business in life was to fight and eat snakes. Nag knew that too, and at the bottom of his cold heart he was afraid.

"Well," said Rikki-tikki, and his tail began to fluff up again, "marks or no marks, do you think it is right for you to eat fledglings out of a nest?"

Nag was thinking to himself, and watching the least little movement in the grass behind Rikki-tikki. He knew that mongooses in the garden meant death sooner or later for him and his family, but he wanted to get Rikki-tikki off his guard. So he dropped his head a little, and put it on one side.

"Let us talk," he said. "You eat eggs. Why should not I eat birds?"

"Behind you! Look behind you!" sang Darzee.

Rikki-tikki knew better than to waste time in staring. He jumped up in the air as high as he could go, and just under him whizzed by the head of Nagaina, Nag's wicked wife. She had crept up behind him as he was talking, to make an end of him; and he heard her savage hiss as the stroke missed. He came down almost across her back, and if he had been an old mongoose he would have known that then was the time to break her back with one bite; but he was afraid of the terrible lashing return-stroke of the cobra. He bit, indeed, but did not bite long enough, and he jumped clear of the whisking tail, leaving Nagaina torn and angry.

"Wicked, wicked Darzee!" said Nag, lashing up as high as he could reach toward the nest in the thorn-bush; but Darzee had built it out of reach of snakes, and it only swayed to and fro.

Rikki-tikki felt his eyes growing red and hot (when a mongoose's eyes grow red, he is angry), and he sat back on his tail and hind legs like a little kangaroo, and looked all round him, and chattered with rage. But Nag and Nagaina had disappeared into the grass. When a snake misses its stroke, it never says anything or gives any sign of what it means to do next. Rikki-tikki did not care to follow them, for he did not feel sure that he could manage two snakes at once. So he trotted off to the gravel path near the house, and sat down to think. It was a serious matter for him.

If you read the old books of natural history, you will find they say that when the mongoose fights the snake and happens to get bitten, he runs off and eats some herb that cures him. That is not true. The victory is only a matter of quickness of eye and quickness of foot – snake's blow against mongoose's jump – and as no eye can follow the motion of a snake's head when it strikes, that makes things much more wonderful than any magic herb. Rikki-tikki knew he was a young mongoose, and it made him all the more pleased to think that he had managed to escape a blow from behind. It gave him confidence in himself, and when Teddy came running down the path, Rikki-tikki was ready to be petted.

But just as Teddy was stooping, something flinched a little in the dust, and a tiny voice said: "Be careful. I am death!" It was Karait, the dusty brown snakeling that lies for choice on the dusty earth; and his bite is as dangerous as the cobra's. But he is so small that nobody thinks of him, and so he does the more harm to people.

Rikki-tikki's eyes grew red again, and he danced up to Karait with the peculiar rocking, swaying motion that he had inherited from his

family. It looks very funny, but it is so perfectly balanced a gait that you can fly off from it at any angle you please; and in dealing with snakes this is an advantage. If Rikki-tikki had only known, he was doing a much more dangerous thing than fighting Nag, for Karait is so small, and can turn so quickly, that unless Rikki bit him close to the back of the head, he would get the return-stroke in his eye or lip. But Rikki did not know: his eyes were all red, and he rocked back and forth, looking for a good place to hold. Karait struck out. Rikki jumped sideways and tried to run in, but the wicked little dusty grey head lashed within a fraction of his shoulder, and he had to jump over the body, and the head followed his heels close.

Teddy shouted to the house: "Oh, look here! Our mongoose is killing a snake"; and Rikki-tikki heard a scream from Teddy's mother. His father ran out with a stick, but by the time he came up, Karait had lunged out once too far, and Rikki-tikki had sprung, jumped on the snake's back, dropped his head far between his fore-legs, bitten as high up the back as he could get hold, and rolled away. That bite paralysed Karait, and Rikki-tikki was just going to eat him up from the tail, after the custom of his family at dinner, when he remembered that a full meal makes a slow mongoose, and if he wanted all his strength and quickness ready, he must keep himself thin.

He went away for a dust-bath under the castor-oil bushes, while Teddy's father beat the dead Karait. "What is the use of that?" thought Rikki-tikki. "I have settled it all;" and then Teddy's mother picked him up from the dust and hugged him, crying that he had saved Teddy from death, and Teddy's father said that he was a providence, and Teddy looked on with big scared eyes. Rikki-tikki was rather amused at all the fuss, which, of course, he did not understand. Teddy's mother might just as well have petted Teddy for playing in the dust. Rikki was thoroughly enjoying himself.

That night, at dinner, walking to and fro among the wine-glasses on the table, he could have stuffed himself three times over with nice things; but he remembered Nag and Nagaina, and though it was very pleasant to be patted and petted by Teddy's mother, and to sit on Teddy's shoulder, his eyes would get red from time to time, and he would go off into his long war-cry of '*Rikk-tikk-tikki-tikki-tchk!*'

Teddy carried him off to bed, and insisted on Rikki-tikki sleeping under his chin. Rikki-tikki was too well bred to bite or scratch, but as soon as Teddy was asleep he went off for his nightly walk round the house, and in the dark he ran up against Chuchundra, the musk-rat, creeping round by the wall. Chuchundra is a broken-hearted little beast. He whimpers and cheeps all the night, trying to make up his mind to run into the middle of the room, but he never gets there.

"Don't kill me," said Chuchundra, almost weeping. "Rikki-tikki, don't kill me."

"Do you think a snake-killer kills musk-rats?" said Rikki-tikki scornfully.

"Those who kill snakes get killed by snakes," said Chuchundra, more sorrowfully than ever. "And how am I to be sure that Nag won't mistake me for you some dark night?"

"There's not the least danger," said Rikki-tikki; "but Nag is in the garden, and I know you don't go there."

"My cousin Chua, the rat, told me – " said Chuchundra, and then he stopped.

"Told you what?"

"H'sh! Nag is everywhere, Rikki-tikki. You should have talked to Chua in the garden."

"I didn't – so you must tell me. Quick, Chuchundra, or I'll bite you!"

Chuchundra sat down and cried till the tears rolled off his whiskers. "I am a very poor man," he sobbed. "I never had spirit enough to run out into the middle of the room. H'sh! I mustn't tell you anything. Can't you *hear*, Rikki-tikki?"

Rikki-tikki listened. The house was as still as still, but he thought he could just catch the faintest *scratch-scratch* in the world – a noise as faint as that of a wasp walking on a window-pane – the dry scratch of a snake's scales on brickwork.

"That's Nag or Nagaina," he said to himself; "and he is crawling into the bathroom sluice. You're right, Chuchundra; I should have talked to Chua."

He stole off to Teddy's bathroom, but there was nothing there, and then to Teddy's mother's bathroom. At the bottom of the smooth plaster wall there was a brick pulled out to make a sluice for the bathwater, and as Rikki-tikki stole in by the masonry curb where the bath is put, he heard Nag and Nagaina whispering together outside in the moonlight.

"When the house is emptied of people," said Nagaina to her husband, "*he* will have to go away, and then the garden will be our own again. Go in quietly, and remember that the big man who killed Karait is the first one to bite. Then come out and tell me, and we will hunt for Rikki-tikki together."

"But are you sure that there is anything to be gained by killing the people?" said Nag.

"Everything. When there were no people in the bungalow, did we have any mongoose in the garden? So long as the bungalow is empty, we are king and queen of the garden; and remember that as soon as our eggs in the melon-bed hatch (as they may tomorrow), our children will need room and quiet."

"I had not thought of that," said Nag. "I will go, but there is no need that we should hunt for Rikki-tikki afterward. I will kill the big man and his wife, and the child if I can, and come away quietly. Then the bungalow will be empty, and Rikki-tikki will go."

Rikki-tikki tingled all over with rage and hatred at this, and then Nag's head came through the sluice, and his five feet of cold body followed it. Angry as he was, Rikki-tikki was very frightened as he saw the size of the big cobra. Nag coiled himself up, raised his head, and looked into the bathroom in the dark, and Rikki could see his eyes glitter.

"Now, if I kill him here, Nagaina will know; and if I fight him on the open floor, the odds are in his favor. What am I to do?" said Rikki-tikki-tavi.

Nag waved to and fro, and then Rikki-tikki heard him drinking from the biggest water-jar that was used to fill the bath. "That is good," said the snake. "Now, when Karait was killed, the big man had a stick. He may have that stick still, but when he comes in to bathe in the morning he will not have a stick. I shall wait here till he comes. Nagaina – do you hear me? – I shall wait here in the cool till daytime."

There was no answer from outside, so Rikki-tikki knew Nagaina had gone away. Nag coiled himself down, coil by coil, round the bulge at the bottom of the water-jar, and Rikki-tikki stayed still as death. After an hour, he began to move, muscle by muscle, toward the jar. Nag was asleep, and Rikki-tikki looked at his big back, wondering which would be the best place for a good hold. "If I don't break his back at the first jump," said Rikki, "he can still fight; and if he fights – oh, Rikki!" He looked at the thickness of the neck below the hood, but that was too much for him; and a bite near the tail would only make Nag savage.

"It must be the head," he said at last; "the head above the hood; and when I am once there, I must not let go."

Then he jumped. The head was lying a little clear of the water-jar, under the curve of it; and, as his teeth met, Rikki braced his back against the bulge of the red earthenware to hold down the head. This gave him just one second's purchase, and he made the most of it. Then he was battered to and fro as a rat is shaken by a dog – to and fro on the floor, up and down, and round in great circles; but his eyes were red, and he held on as the body cart-whipped over the floor, upsetting the tin dipper and the soap-dish and the flesh-brush, and banged against the tin side of the bath. As he held he closed his jaws tighter and tighter, for he made sure he would be banged to death, and, for the honor of his family, he preferred to be found with his teeth locked. He was dizzy, aching, and felt shaken to pieces when something went off like a thunderclap just behind him; a hot wind knocked him senseless, and red fire singed his fur. The big man had been wakened by the noise, and had fired both barrels of a shotgun into Nag just behind the hood.

Rikki-tikki held on with his eyes shut, for now he was quite sure he was dead; but the head did not move, and the big man picked him up and said: "It's our mongoose again, Alice; the little chap has saved *our* lives now." Then Teddy's mother came in with a very white face, and saw what was left of Nag, and Rikki-tikki dragged himself to Teddy's bedroom and spent half the rest of the night shaking himself tenderly to find out whether he really was broken into forty pieces, as he fancied.

When morning came he was very stiff, but well pleased with his doings. "Now I have Nagaina to settle with, and she will be worse than five Nags, and there's no knowing when the eggs she spoke of will hatch. Goodness! I must go and see Darzee," he said.

Without waiting for breakfast, Rikki-tikki ran to the thorn-bush where Darzee was singing a song of triumph at the top of his voice. The news of Nag's death was all over the garden, for the sweeper had thrown the body on the rubbish-heap.

"Oh, you stupid tuft of feathers!" said Rikki-tikki angrily. "Is this the time to sing?"

"Nag is dead – is dead – is dead!" sang Darzee. "The valiant Rikki-tikki caught him by the head and held fast. The big man brought the bang-stick, and Nag fell in two pieces! He will never eat my babies again."

"All that's true enough; but where's Nagaina?" said Rikki-tikki, looking carefully round him.

"Nagaina came to the bathroom sluice and called for Nag," Darzee went on; "and Nag came out on the end of a stick – the sweeper picked him up on the end of a stick and threw him upon the rubbish-heap. Let us sing about the great, the red-eyed Rikki-tikki!" and Darzee filled his throat and sang.

"If I could get up to your nest, I'd roll all your babies out!" said Rikki-tikki. "You don't know when to do the right thing at the right time. You're safe enough in your nest there, but it's war for me down here. Stop singing a minute, Darzee."

"For the great, the beautiful Rikki-tikki's sake I will stop," said Darzee. "What is it, O Killer of the terrible Nag?"

"Where is Nagaina, for the third time?"

"On the rubbish-heap by the stables, mourning for Nag. Great is Rikki-tikki with the white teeth."

"Bother my white teeth! Have you ever heard where she keeps her eggs?"

"In the melon-bed, on the end nearest the wall, where the sun strikes nearly all day. She hid them there weeks ago."

"And you never thought it worth while to tell me? The end nearest the wall you said?"

"Rikki-tikki, you are not going to eat her eggs?"

"Not eat exactly; no. Darzee, if you have a grain of sense you will fly off to the stables and pretend that your wing is broken, and let Nagaina chase you away to this bush. I must get to the melon-bed, and if I went there now she'd see me."

Darzee was a feather-brained little fellow who could never hold more than one idea at a time in his head; and just because he knew that Nagaina's children were born in eggs like his own, he didn't think at first that it was fair to kill them. But his wife was a sensible bird, and she knew that cobra's eggs meant young cobras later on; so she flew off from the nest, and left Darzee to keep the babies warm, and continue his song about the death of Nag. Darzee was very like a man in some ways.

She fluttered in front of Nagaina by the rubbish-heap, and cried out: "Oh, my wing is broken! The boy in the house threw a stone at me and broke it." Then she fluttered more desperately then ever.

Nagaina lifted up her head and hissed: "You warned Rikki-tikki when I would have killed him. Indeed and truly, you've chosen a bad place to be lame in." And she moved toward Darzee's wife, slipping along over the dust.

"The boy broke it with a stone!" shrieked Darzee's wife.

"Well, it may be some consolation to you when you're dead to know that I shall settle accounts with the boy. My husband lies on the rubbish-heap this morning, but before night the boy in the house will lie very still. What is the use of running away? I am sure to catch you.

Little fool, look at me!"

Darzee's wife knew better than to do *that*, for a bird who looks at a snake's eyes gets so frightened that she cannot move. Darzee's wife fluttered on, piping sorrowfully, and never leaving the ground, and Nagaina quickened her pace.

Rikki-tikki heard them going up the path from the stables, and he raced for the end of the melon-patch near the wall. There, in the warm litter about the melons, very cunningly hidden, he found twenty-five eggs, about the size of a bantam's eggs, but with whitish skin instead of shell.

"I was not a day too soon," he said: for he could see the baby cobras curled up inside the skin, and he knew that the minute they were hatched they could each kill a man or a mongoose. He bit off the tops of the eggs as fast as he could, taking care to crush the young cobras, and turned over the litter from time to time to see whether he had missed any. At last there were only three eggs left, and Rikki-tikki began to chuckle to himself, when he heard Darzee's wife screaming:

"Rikki-tikki, I led Nagaina toward the house, and she has gone into the veranda, and – oh, come quickly – she means killing!"

Rikki-tikki smashed two eggs, and tumbled backward down the melon-bed with the third egg in his mouth, and scuttled to the veranda as hard as he could put foot to the ground. Teddy and his mother and father were there at early breakfast; but Rikki-tikki saw that they were not eating anything. They sat stone-still, and their faces were white. Nagaina was coiled up on the matting by Teddy's chair, within easy striking-distance of Teddy's bare leg, and she was swaying to and fro singing a song of triumph.

"Son of the big man that killed Nag," she hissed, "stay still, I am not ready yet. Wait a little. Keep very still, all you three. If you move I strike, and if you do not move I strike. Oh, foolish people, who killed my Nag!"

Teddy's eyes were fixed on his father, and all his father could do was to whisper: "Sit still, Teddy. You mustn't move. Teddy, keep still."

Then Rikki-tikki came up and cried: "Turn round, Nagaina; turn and fight!"

"All in good time," said she, without moving her eyes. "I will settle my account with *you* presently. Look at your friends, Rikki-tikki. They are still and white; they are afraid. They dare not move, and if you come a step nearer I strike."

"Look at your eggs," said Rikki-tikki, "in the melon-bed near the wall. Go and look, Nagaina."

The big snake turned half round, and saw the egg on the veranda. "Ah-h! Give it to me," she said.

Rikki-tikki put his paws one on each side of the egg, and his eyes were blood-red. "What price for a snake's egg? For a young cobra? For a young king-cobra? For the last – the very last of the brood? The ants are eating all the others down by the melon-bed."

Nagaina spun clear round, forgetting everything for the sake of the one egg; and Rikki-tikki saw Teddy's father shoot out a big hand, catch Teddy by the shoulder, and drag him across the little table with the tea-cups, safe and out of reach of Nagaina.

"Tricked! Tricked! Tricked! *Rikk-tck-tck!*" chuckled Rikki-tikki. "The boy is safe, and it was I – I – I that caught Nag by the hood last night in the bathroom." Then he began to jump up and down, all four feet together, his head close to the floor. "He threw me to and fro, but he could not shake me off. He was dead before the big man blew him in two. I did it. *Rikki-tikki-tck-tck!* Come then, Nagaina. Come and fight with me. You shall not be a widow long."

Nagaina saw that she had lost her chance of killing Teddy, and the egg lay between Rikki-tikki's paws. "Give me the egg, Rikki-tikki. Give me the last of my eggs, and I will go away and never come back," she said, lowering her hood.

"Yes, you will go away, and you will never come back; for you will go to the rubbish-heap with Nag. Fight, widow! The big man has gone for his gun! Fight!"

Rikki-tikki was bounding all round Nagaina, keeping just out of reach of her stroke, his little eyes like hot coals. Nagaina gathered herself together, and flung out at him. Rikki-tikki jumped up and backward. Again and again and again she struck, and each time her head came with a whack on the matting of the veranda, and she gathered herself together like a watch-spring. Then Rikki-tikki danced in a circle to get behind her, and Nagaina spun round to keep her head to his head, so that the rustle of her tail on the matting sounded like dry leaves blown along by the wind.

He had forgotten the egg. It still lay on the veranda, and Nagaina came nearer and nearer to it, till at last, while Rikki-tikki was drawing breath, she caught it in her mouth, turned to the veranda steps, and flew like an arrow down the path, with Rikki-tikki behind her. When the cobra runs for her life, she goes like a whiplash flicked across a horse's neck.

Rikki-tikki knew that he must catch her, or all the trouble would begin again. She headed straight for the long grass by the thorn-bush, and as he was running Rikki-tikki heard Darzee still singing his foolish little song of triumph. But Darzee's wife was wiser. She flew off her nest as Nagaina came along, and flapped her wings about Nagaina's head. If Darzee had helped they might have turned her; but Nagaina only lowered her hood and went on. Still the instant's delay brought

The four friends let loose a shrieking and a squalling fit to wake the dead
(*The Musicians of Bremen*)

"You'll stay to supper, Brer Fox?" (*Brer Rabbit's Good Children*)

". . . I'm very popular with all the family." (*The Dog and the Wolf*)

"What a journey!" (*The City Mouse and the Country Mouse*)

Rikki-tikki up to her, and as she plunged into the rat-hole where she and Nag used to live, his little white teeth were clenched on her tail, and he went down with her – and very few mongooses, however wise and old they may be, care to follow a cobra into its hole. It was dark in the hole; and Rikki-tikki never knew when it might open out and give Nagaina room to turn and strike at him. He held on savagely, and stuck out his feet to act as brakes on the dark slope of the hot, moist earth.

Then the grass by the mouth of the hole stopped waving, and Darzee said, "It is all over with Rikki-tikki! We must sing his death-song. Valiant Rikki-tikki is dead! For Nagaina will surely kill him underground."

So he sang a very mournful song that he made up on the spur of the minute, and just as he got to the most touching part the grass quivered again, and Rikki-tikki, covered with dirt, dragged himself out of the hole leg by leg, licking his whiskers. Darzee stopped with a little shout. Rikki-tikki shook some of the dust out of his fur and sneezed. "It is all over," he said. "The widow will never come out again." And the red ants that live between the grass-stems heard him, and began to troop down one after another to see if he had spoken the truth.

Rikki-tikki curled himself up in the grass and slept where he was – slept and slept till it was late in the afternoon, for he had done a hard day's work.

"Now," he said, when he awoke, "I will go back to the house. Tell the Coppersmith, Darzee, and he will tell the garden that Nagaina is dead."

The Coppersmith is a bird who makes a noise exactly like the beating of a little hammer on a copper pot; and the reason he is always making it is because he is the town-crier to every Indian garden, and

tells all the news to everybody who cares to listen. As Rikki-tikki went up the path, he heard his "attention" notes like a tiny dinner-gong; and then the steady "*Ding-dong-tock!* Nag is dead – *dong!* Nagaina is dead! *Ding-dong-tock!*" That set all the birds in the garden singing, and the frogs croaking; for Nag and Nagaina used to eat frogs as well as little birds.

When Rikki got to the house, Teddy and Teddy's mother (she still looked very white, for she had been fainting) and Teddy's father came out and almost cried over him; and that night he ate all that was given him till he could eat no more, and went to bed on Teddy's shoulder, where Teddy's mother saw him when she came to look late at night.

"He saved our lives and Teddy's life," she said to her husband. "Just think, he saved all our lives!"

Rikki-tikki woke up with a jump, for all the mongooses are light sleepers.

"Oh, it's you," said he. "What are you bothering for? All the cobras are dead; and if they weren't, I'm here."

Rikki-tikki had a right to be proud of himself; but he did not grow too proud, and he kept that garden as a mongoose should keep it, with tooth and jump and spring and bite, till never a cobra dared show its head inside the walls.


## Darzee's Chant
### (SUNG IN HONOR OF RIKKI-TIKKI-TAVI)

Singer and tailor am I –
  Doubled the joys that I know –
Proud of my lilt through the sky,

Proud of the house that I sew —
Over and under, so weave I my music — so weave I the house
that I sew.

Sing to your fledglings again,
Mother, oh, lift up your head!
Evil that plagues us is slain,
Death in the garden lies dead.
Terror that hid in the roses is impotent — flung on the dung-hill
and dead!

Who hath delivered us, who?
Tell me his nest and his name.
Rikki, the valiant, the true,
Tikki, with eyeballs of flame,
Rik-tikki-tikki, the ivory-fangèd, the hunter with eyeballs of
flame.

Give him the Thanks of the Birds,
Blowing with tail-feathers spread!
Praise him with nightingale-words —
Nay, I will praise him instead.
Hear! I will sing you the praise of the bottle-tailed Rikki, with
eyeballs of red!

*(Here Rikki-tikki interrupted, and the rest of the song is lost.)*

# THE TOMTIT AND THE BEAR

The Brothers Grimm

ONE FINE summer day the wolf and the bear were walking together in a wood, when they heard a bird singing most beautifully.

"Brother," said the bear, "what kind of bird is that?"

"Oh," said the wolf, "that's the King of the Birds. We must be very respectful to him."

(The bird was actually the tomtit, though the wolf and the bear didn't know this.)

"Well," said the bear, "I'd like to see the royal palace. Come and show me where it is."

"Not yet," said the wolf. "We must wait until the Queen comes home."

Soon the Queen – who was of course the mother tomtit – arrived with food in her beak for her young. Both the father and the mother tomtit began to feed their children.

"Let's have a look at this palace," said the bear.

"No, no," said the wolf. "We must wait until they've gone."

So they marked the place where they'd seen the nest and then went away. But the bear was so anxious to see the royal palace that they soon returned. The bear peeped into the tomtit's nest and there he saw the five or six young birds.

"This isn't a royal palace!" he exclaimed in disgust. "I never saw such a filthy place! And these aren't royal children. They're just scruffy little brats!"

When the young tomtits heard this, they cried out, "We are not scruffy brats! Our mother and father are good, honest people. Just you wait, you'll suffer for this!"

Then the wolf and the bear took fright and ran away. When the parent birds returned to the nest with food for their children, the

young ones refused to eat. "We won't touch a thing," they said, "not until that wicked bear has been punished for insulting us."

"You can rest easy," said their father. "He will be punished. I promise."

So the father tomtit went out and stood in front of the bear's den and cried out, "You have insulted our children. Therefore, we hereby declare war on you, and we will fight until you've been punished as you deserve."

When the bear heard this, he called the ox, the ass, the stag and all the beasts of the earth to come and defend him. On his side, the tomtit called together the birds of the air and a very large army of hornets, gnats, bees, flies, and other insects.

Before the war began, the tomtit sent out spies to find out who was commander-in-chief of the enemy's forces. The gnat was the cleverest spy of all. He flew backwards and forwards in the wood where the enemy camped and hid under a leaf so that he could hear everything when the orders were being given out.

He heard the bear call to the fox, "Reynard, you are the cleverest of all the animals. You shall be our general and lead us into battle. But first, we must agree on a signal, so that we'll know what you want us to do."

"Look," said the fox. "I have a fine long bushy tail, like a plume of feathers. Now, remember: when you see me raise my tail, you'll know we have won the battle. All you have to do is rush down on the enemy. But if I drop my tail, then we've lost, and you must run away as fast as you can."

The gnat heard all this and flew back to tell the tomtit.

The day of the battle arrived, and the army of animals rushed forward with such a fearful sound that the earth shook. The tomtit and the other birds and all the insects flew into battle looking very warlike, flapping and fluttering and beating the air with their wings.

Then the tomtit ordered the troop of hornets to fly towards the fox and to sting him as hard as they could on the tail. The hornets did as they were told. When the fox felt the first sting he flinched, but he was very brave and kept his tail up. The second sting made him drop his tail for a moment. But when the third hornet stung him, he dropped his tail and ran away as fast as he could.

When the animals saw the fox had dropped his tail, they thought this was a signal. They had lost the battle! So they too ran away. The King and Queen tomtit flew back triumphantly to their children. "We've won! We've won!" they cried. "Now, children, you can eat and drink as much as you like."

"No," said the young birds. "Not until the bear has humbly begged our pardon."

So the King tomtit flew back to the bear's den. "Come out!" he cried. "Come back to my home. You must beg my children to forgive you – or every bone in your body will be broken!"

The bear crawled out of his den in a very sulky way, and did as he was told. Then the young birds sat down and ate and drank and celebrated late into the night.

# THE CAT
# AND THE FOX

La Fontaine

THE CAT and the fox were friends, but like lots of friends, they argued a great deal. They argued who ran the faster, who was the more handsome, who had the better voice.

One day the fox said to the cat, "I'm going on a journey. Do you want to come with me?"

"Yes, I'll come," said the cat, and they spent a good hour arguing about the plans for the journey. They argued about the food they should take with them – bread, cheese or meat? But at last they packed up the food. Then they argued about the way they should take. But at last they managed to agree. And so they set off.

As they walked along the road, they still argued. They paid no attention to the trees and flowers around them, or the blue sky up above.

"I am much cleverer than you," said the fox.

It was an argument they had had many times before.

"No, you're not," said the cat.

"Oh, yes, I am," said the fox.

"Tell me how," said the cat scornfully.

"Well," said the fox, "I know a hundred clever tricks."

"Ha! Ha!" scoffed the cat. "I know just one trick. But my trick is a thousand times better than all of yours."

They had been so busy arguing that they hadn't noticed that the way led through a deep, dark forest. Suddenly, from behind the trees, there were shouts, and a group of hunters with their dogs rushed forward.

Immediately the cat climbed to the top of a tall pine tree. There he clung on to a branch and looked down at the men and dogs.

"It's no use," said one. "We can't reach the cat." So instead they went after the fox.

"I'll be sure to escape," he said to himself. "I know a hundred clever tricks."

So he dodged this way and that, through the thickets and behind the trees, but the hounds were too fast for him.

At last he hid in a hole, but he could still hear the dogs above ground. "I can't stay here," he said to himself, and he jumped out of the hole into the air – and immediately the dogs rushed forward and caught him.

"Poor fox!" said the cat sadly, as he looked down from his branch at the top of the tall tree.

The moral of this story is – when in danger it is better to have one really good way of escape than a great many which are not so good.

# THE MUSICIANS OF BREMEN

## The Brothers Grimm

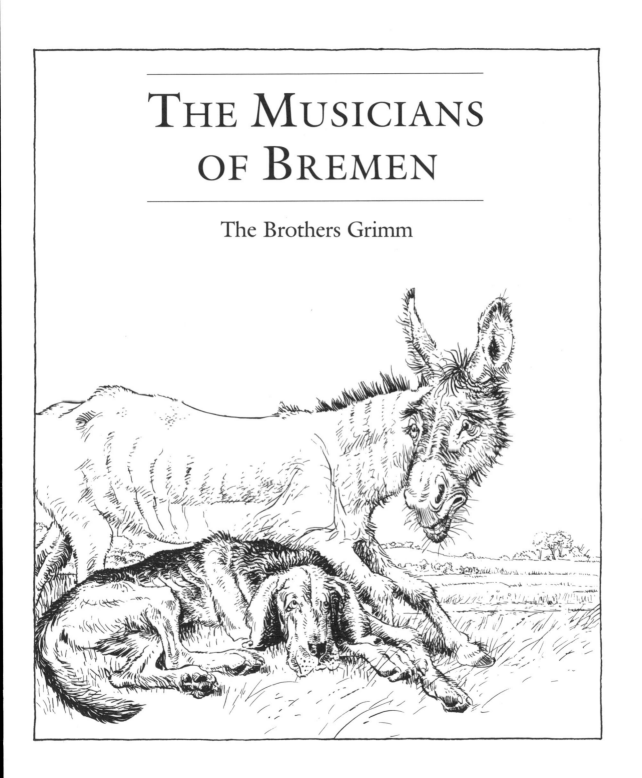

ONCE UPON a time there lived a farmer who was extremely mean. He had an ass who had been a faithful servant to him for many years, but who was now growing old and less fit for work. The farmer was tired of keeping him and feeding him, and began to think of putting an end to the faithful ass.

But the ass knew what his master was planning, and he decided to leave before it was too late. One morning, he managed to push back the latch of his miserable old stable and set off towards the great city of Bremen. "I've still got my voice," he said to himself, "even though I'm old. I might become a musician."

He hadn't gone far before he met a dog lying on a patch of grass by the crossroads. The dog's tongue was hanging out, and he was panting fit to burst.

"What's wrong, my friend?" asked the ass.

"I've run away," replied the dog. "I've served my master well for twelve years, but just because I'm getting old and was no use to him, he was going to knock me over the head. Luckily I escaped." He sighed. "I'm too old to work. Look at me! What can I do? I'm finished."

"No, you're not!" said the ass. "Nonsense! I'm in just the same position as you. My master was like yours. But I'm off to Bremen to be a town musician. Why don't you come with me?"

"All right," said the dog, and off they went together. They had gone only a few miles and had reached the last thatched house in a little village when they saw a cat. She was sitting hunched up on the red brick wall of an old orchard, looking utterly dejected.

"What's wrong?" asked the ass. "You look miserable."

"Well," said the cat, "it isn't easy to be cheerful when your life's in danger. Just because I'm getting old and would rather sit by the fire than go chasing mice, my mistress tried to drown me in the water butt. I managed to escape, but what do I do now? I can't earn a living at my age."

"Well, that's a sad story," said the ass. "But you've still got a sweet voice. Come with us. We're off to Bremen to be musicians – we're going to make our fortune. Do come with us."

The cat thought this was a splendid idea. She leapt down from the wall and off they all went together.

Not long after this, as they were passing a busy farmyard, they saw a cock perched on a five-barred gate, screeching out his cock-a-doodle-doo as if with his last breath.

"What a noise you're making!" cried the ass. "What's it all about?"

"Just a few minutes ago," said the cock, "I was telling my mistress, the farmer's wife, and her fat cook that we'd have fine weather for washday. Did I get a word of thanks? No! They threatened to chop my head off in the morning and make me into a broth for their visitors on Sunday."

"Broth, indeed!" said the ass. "We can't have that. You come along with us. We're going to the city of Bremen. If we all sing in time and in tune, we might be able to give a concert. Let's be off to make our fortunes!"

The cock agreed willingly, and so off they went. But they still had many miles to travel, and they couldn't reach the city that evening. So when night fell, they went into a wood to sleep. The ass and the dog settled down under the branches of an oak. The cat climbed up into the tree, and the cock flew to the topmost branch where he thought he'd be safe. Before he went to sleep he looked around him to see that all was well, and there, in the distance, he saw a light.

He called down to his friends, "I can see a bright shining light.

There must be a house somewhere near."

"Well," said the ass, "any roof is better than none. Let's go and find it."

"I could do with a fine juicy bone," added the dog as they set out.

They made their way towards the light, and soon they found themselves beside the walls of an old house. This house was the secret haunt of a wild and dangerous band of robbers, but the four friends didn't know this.

The ass was the tallest of the animals, so he stepped up to the window and peeped in.

"What can you see?" asked the cock.

"I can see a long table spread with gold and silver plates and a feast fit for a king. But I don't like the look of the company. They're a wicked-looking lot, I can tell you."

"This would make a fine house for *us*," said the cat, her whiskers twitching. "And the food smells good."

"If only the house were empty and we could get inside," said the ass.

So the animals fell to discussing how they could get the robbers out of the house and themselves safely in.

At last they had an idea. The ass stood on his hind legs, his forefeet against the windowsill; the dog leapt on to his back; the cat scrambled on to the dog's shoulders; and the cock perched on the cat's head.

At a signal from the ass, the four friends let loose a shrieking and a squalling fit to wake the dead. The ass brayed, the dog barked, the cat miaowed and the cock screeched.

Then suddenly they went tumbling through the window with a crash and a bang and a smashing of broken glass. The robbers, already scared out of their wits by the noise, thought that demons had broken in. They leapt from their chairs and rushed out of the house into the darkness, without so much as a backward glance.

Once the robbers had gone, the four friends sat down at the table and ate and drank till they couldn't eat any more. Then they puffed out the candles and settled down to rest.

The ass stretched out on a heap of straw in the yard; the dog lay down on a mat behind the door; the cat curled up on the warm ashes in the hearth; and the cock perched on the chimneypot. They were all soon asleep.

About midnight, the robbers, watching from a distance, saw that all the lights were out and they began to wonder why they had been in such a hurry to run away. One of the robbers, braver than the rest, crept up to the house. Nothing stirred as he made his way to the back porch and into the kitchen.

As he was groping about the kitchen in the pitch dark, trying to find a candle, he saw the glittering eyes of the cat, and mistook them for live coals.

He bent down and picked up a splinter of wood, and held it towards them for a light. In a flash the cat sprang at him, spitting and swearing. He stumbled backwards in the dark, bruising his shins and his elbows, and tried to make his way to the back door. There he tumbled over the dog, who leapt up with a growl and bit him hard on the leg.

He fell out of the door into the yard and tripped over the ass, who gave him a great kick with his hind leg. All this noise was enough to wake the cock, who lifted up his head, flapped his wings and screeched loudly.

The robber was terrified. He ran back as fast as his bruised bones

would let him to the other robbers waiting in the wood. "There's an evil old creature in there!" he gasped. "She screamed and spat at me, and scratched my cheek with her long talons. I'd no sooner fought her off, than a demon with a long sharp knife stabbed me in the leg. A huge black creature lying in wait in the yard felled me with his club. Then the devil himself, up on the chimney top, cried out, 'Hey! Cut the rascal into a million pieces!' "

When they heard this, the robbers were so afraid that they never went back to the house – in fact, they were never seen in the woods again.

The four friends were so pleased with their fine house and all the treasures inside that they decided to stay there. "We needn't go any further," they said. Sometimes, in the evening, you can hear strange and happy music coming from the house.

And unless they've gone to Bremen, the four friends are still there today.

# BRER RABBIT'S
# GOOD CHILDREN

Joel Chandler Harris

BRER RABBIT'S children were very good children. They always did just what they were told. When Mrs. Rabbit said "Scoot!" they scooted. And when Brer Rabbit said, "Come here, children," all the little rabbits obeyed him at once. They kept their clothes clean and they ate up every scrap of their dinner.

One day the wicked Brer Fox dropped in to see Brer Rabbit. But Brer Rabbit wasn't at home. He had gone out hunting. Mrs. Rabbit wasn't at home either. She had gone to a sewing party with her friends.

"Where's your father?" said Brer Fox, with a cunning glint in his eye.

"He's gone out," said the little rabbits.

"And where's your mother?" asked the fox.

"She's gone out too," said the rabbits.

"Ah . . . ," said the wicked Brer Fox, and he licked his lips. He settled himself in Brer Rabbit's best chair.

Then he spotted a stalk of sugarcane in the corner of the kitchen.

"Break off a piece of that sugarcane for me," he ordered the little rabbits.

Now Brer Rabbit's children always did what they were told, so they all tried very hard to break the sugarcane. But it was much too hard for them.

They puffed and panted and struggled, but they couldn't break it.

"Hurry up!" snarled the fox. "I'm getting hungry."

Suddenly, from the rooftop of the house, a little bird began to sing. It sang:

> "Take your teeth and gnaw it.
> Take your teeth and saw it."

The little rabbits heard the bird and they started gnawing the sugar-cane. Soon they were able to break off a piece quite easily.

"Good," said Brer Fox, as he crunched the sugarcane. He smiled in his cunning way, for he had thought of another trick to play on the little rabbits.

"I'm thirsty," he said. "Bring me a drink of water." He chortled to himself. "Take that sieve and bring me some fresh water from the pail."

The little rabbits, who always did what they were told, took the sieve and carried it to the pail of water. But as soon as they filled the sieve with water, the water ran out again.

"I'm waiting!" roared the fox.

"Oh dear, he's getting angry. What can we do?" The little rabbits gazed in dismay as the water ran through the holes.

But again the little bird began to sing.

> "Fill it with moss and daub it with clay.
> The fox will get madder, the longer you stay."

What a good idea! The little rabbits ran to gather moss and mud. They filled the sieve with moss, then daubed it with mud so that the water didn't run out. Then they ran back to the fox and gave him a drink of water from the sieve.

"I'm cold," said the fox. "Brrr . . ." He pretended to shiver and shake. "Bring me a big stick of wood and I'll put it on the fire."

He pointed to a very large stick. "Bring me that stick by the door."

The little rabbits were very tired by now, and they just couldn't move the big stick. But, for the third time, the little bird came to their rescue and started to sing.

"Spit on your hands and roll it, try:
Push and shove and you'll get by."

Then the little bird flew away. The rabbits began to do as he had told them. They rolled the big stick of wood to the fire, and the fox picked it up and put it on the grate.

By now the fox had almost run out of ideas. He hoped that the little rabbits would be so tired that they wouldn't run away. Then he could catch them easily.

"Ah . . . ," he yawned, looking at them out of his cunning old eyes. He was just about to pounce when the door opened and in walked Brer Rabbit.

"Hallo, Brer Fox!" he said. "I didn't expect to find you here."

He turned to the little rabbits. "Hallo, children! Have you been good?"

"Oh, yes, Father," they all said. "We've fetched sugarcane and a drink of water and a big stick for the fire, just as Mr. Fox told us."

"Did you now?" said Brer Rabbit. He knew that the wily Brer Fox was up to no good. "You'll stay to supper, Brer Fox?" he said. "I feel kind of lonely tonight. I could do with your company."

Brer Fox knew very well that the game was up. Brer Rabbit was sure to play a trick on him.

"No, thank you," he said. Brer Rabbit and the family of little rabbits were much too clever for him. "No," he gulped. "I've got to be off."

And he rushed out of the door and ran away, just as fast as his paws could carry him.

# THE SPARROWS' TUG-OF-WAR

### West African Folk Tale

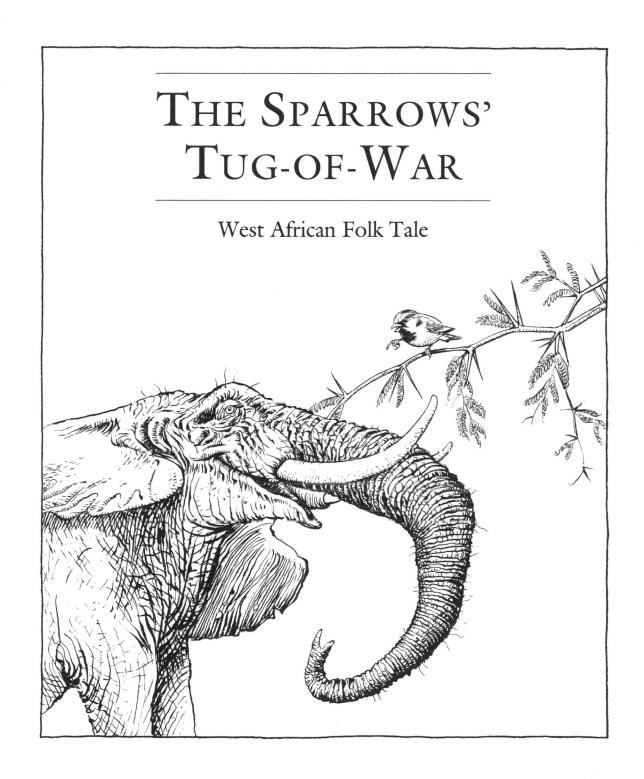

ONE SUMMER morning Mother Sparrow was sitting on her nestful of eggs, enjoying the bright summer sunshine. She could hear the other birds chirping merrily away among the trees and the monkeys chattering for all their worth. In fact everything would have been perfect but for one thing – Father Sparrow was cross, very cross.

"It's that ugly old crocodile," he grumbled. "I went down to bathe in that nice shallow part of the river, you know, and there he was, spread out all over the place. No room for me at all! And when I very politely told him off, he opened his big mouth and laughed. And do you know what he said? 'Go away,' he said, 'I shall stay here as long as I please. Go and have your dip somewhere else.'"

Just as Father Sparrow was speaking, there was a sudden tremendous bump against the tree which tipped him off his twig and very nearly flung Mother Sparrow out of her nest. Father Sparrow flew up to see who it was. It was none other than Brother Elephant, taking his morning constitutional. "Hey there, Brother Elephant," called out Father Sparrow with a furious chirrup. "D'you realize that you've nearly shaken my missus out of her nest?"

"Well, what of that, there's no harm done," answered Brother Elephant, without even apologizing.

"No harm done indeed! You've given her the shock of her life. I warn you, Brother Elephant, if you ever do that again, *I'll tie you up!*"

Brother Elephant gave a mighty guffaw. "Ho! Ho! Ho! Tie me up indeed! Go ahead, Father Sparrow. You and all the other sparrows. You are perfectly welcome to tie me up. *But you won't keep me tied.* Neither you nor all the sparrows in the whole wide world." And off he stamped, still guffawing.

"We'll see about that," twittered Father Sparrow, his feathers all a-fluff. Still furiously angry, he flew down to the river where he found the crocodile still all a-sprawl, sunning himself in the nice shallow part of the river.

"I give you warning, Crocodile," chirped Father Sparrow sternly (whereupon the crocodile lazily opened one eye), "that if you are not out of this place by tomorrow morning, *I shall tie you up*."

"Tie me up as much as you like," answered the crocodile, closing his eye, "and welcome to it. *But you can't keep me tied* – neither you nor all the sparrows in the whole wide world."

"We'll see about that," said Father Sparrow and, whisking his tail, he flew back to Mother Sparrow.

All the rest of the day he was very busy discussing matters with all the other sparrows in the forest. And in the afternoon, several hundreds of them got together and, working very hard, they finally made a long length of creeper, very thick and very stout – as strong as any rope.

Soon Brother Elephant came crashing through the forest and, *Doying!* came bump against Father Sparrow's tree.

"And now what are you going to do, Father Sparrow?" asked Brother Elephant. "Ready to tie me up, eh?"

"Yes, we are," replied Father Sparrow. And he and all his friends flew up and round and round and down and up again with the long creeper-rope between their beaks, till it was all tightly bound round Brother Elephant's enormous body.

"Now listen to me, Brother Elephant," said Father Sparrow, "when I give the word 'PULL,' pull as hard as you can."

"Rightee-ho," answered Brother Elephant, guffawing and shaking with laughter.

But all the sparrows had flown away with the other end of the creeper-rope, pulling it through bush and tree, till they came to the river where Crocodile was.

"So you've come to tie me up, Father Sparrow?" he asked, opening a lazy eye.

"Yes, that's exactly what we *are* going to do," came the reply.

"Tie away," said Crocodile and the sparrows set to work pecking and tugging, flying up and down and up and down again and again and round and round, till the rope was tight and firm round Crocodile's long, slimy body.

"Now," said Father Sparrow, "when I say 'PULL,' don't forget, *pull*."

"Right," said Crocodile, half asleep, and the sparrows whisked their tails and flew off.

Then Father Sparrow perched himself in the middle of the creeper-rope where neither Brother Elephant nor Crocodile could see him (and neither of *them* could see the other), and then, IN A VERY LOUD CHIRP, he called "PULL."

You can well imagine Crocodile's surprise when he found himself jerked out of his sleep and halfway up the river bank. You can also imagine Brother Elephant's astonishment when, a couple of seconds later, *he* found himself pulled off his feet – by Crocodile tugging back. Of course, they both thought it was Father Sparrow who was pulling them.

"What a mighty sparrow!" thought Brother Elephant.

"That little bird certainly knows how to pull!" thought Crocodile.

And so now the tug-of-war began in earnest. They each pulled with all their might and main. Sometimes Brother Elephant would gain the upper hand for a few minutes and Crocodile would be dragged up the river bank. Sometimes Crocodile would pull more strongly and

Brother Elephant would have to dig his big feet into the earth to stop himself being pulled over. The contest was pretty even, and it went on and on with both of them puffing and panting and groaning, and all the sparrows watching from up above twittered and laughed and enjoyed themselves hugely.

Towards evening, when the sun was beginning to set, Crocodile said to himself, "I'd better not let the other animals see me in this state when they come down to drink at the river." So he called out: "Oh, please, Father Sparrow, please stop tugging and untie me. I promise never to take your bathing place again."

And Brother Elephant cried out in a tiny trumpet: "Father Sparrow, if you stop pulling and untie me, I promise I will never bump into your tree again."

"Oh, very well," said Father Sparrow, "very well."

And so all the sparrows set to work again, hopping and pulling and pecking and chattering, until they had untied Crocodile, who then slid, shamefaced, into the river among the tall reeds and hid himself until it was pitch dark. Then they went and did the same thing to Brother Elephant who then trod quietly away (almost on tiptoe!), thoroughly ashamed of being beaten by such a tiny bird. And all the sparrows, satisfied with their day's work, whisked their tails and flew away.

And Father Sparrow was now able to live in peace and take his dip in his favorite shallow part of the river. And Mother Sparrow was able to sit quietly on her nest of eggs.

# THE DOG
# AND THE WOLF

Æsop

ONE MOONLIT night, a lean, hungry, half-starved wolf happened to come across a jolly, plump, well-fed dog. When they had greeted one another, the wolf said:

"I must say, you're looking extremely well. I never saw anyone so radiant and healthy. Tell me, how is it that you live so much better than I do? No one is braver or more willing to work than I am, and yet I'm almost dying of hunger."

"Why," answered the dog, "you could live just as well as me, if you were willing to do what I do."

"And what is that?" asked the wolf.

"Oh," said the dog, "simply guard the house at night and keep the thieves away."

"Gladly," replied the wolf, "for I'm having a hard time of it at present. Some good food and a warm roof over my head would be very welcome after the cold wet woods where I'm living now."

"Come along with me then," said the dog.

Now, as they were trotting along together, the wolf noticed a mark on the dog's neck and couldn't resist asking him what it was.

"Oh, it's nothing," said the dog.

"No, do tell me," the wolf insisted.

"Well, if you must know," replied the dog, "I'm tied up in the daytime, because I'm quite fierce and they're afraid that I might bite people. But they do it to make me sleep during the day, more than anything else, and as soon as it's dark, I'm let out and may go wherever I want. What's more, my master brings me the bones and scraps from the table with his own hands. I get all the leftovers, as I'm very popular with all the family. So there you are – that is how you are to live. Well, come on! What's the matter with you?"

"No, I'm sorry," replied the wolf, "but you may keep your

136

happiness to yourself. Freedom is everything to me. I would not be a king if I had to live in the way you have described."

The moral of the story is this: it is better to be the most humble person on earth, and free, than to be exalted but lose one's independence.

# DICK WHITTINGTON AND HIS CAT

## Traditional English Tale

LONG AGO in England there was a little boy called Dick Whittington whose mother and father had died when he was very young. He was not yet old enough to work, and so he was very poor and seldom had enough to eat. The people in his village were also very poor, so they had no food to give him – sometimes they could spare a few potato peelings and a hard crust of bread, but that was all.

Dick had heard a great deal about the wonderful city of London. There, he was told, lived many grand ladies and gentlemen. There was singing all day long and the streets were paved with gold.

One day a wagon drawn by eight horses with bells at their heads drove through the village. Dick thought that such a wonderful wagon *must* be going to London, so he begged the driver to take him to the great city. The wagon driver, who was a kind man, saw Dick's ragged clothes and thought the boy could not be worse off in the city than he was in the village. He told Dick to climb up beside him and they set off for London together.

When Dick got to London, he was so eager to find the streets paved with gold that he hardly stopped to thank the wagon driver but ran off as fast as he could go. He ran through the streets till he was tired out, but he found only dirt instead of gold, and at last he sat down in a dark corner and fell sound asleep.

Next morning Dick awoke very hungry. He walked about the streets asking everyone he met for a halfpenny to keep him from starving, but everyone seemed in a great hurry and only one or two people gave him any money. Gradually he became weak from lack of food.

At last he lay down on the doorstep of a house belonging to Mr. Fitzwarren, a rich merchant. The cook, a bad-tempered creature, saw him lying there and shouted angrily, "Go away, you lazy rogue, or I'll pour this dishwater over you." She was about to do just that when the merchant returned and saw the poor ragged boy lying on the step. "Why are you lying there?" he asked. "You look as if you're old enough to work."

"I would work, sir," said Dick, "but I know no one in this city and I'm weak for want of food."

"Take him into the house," said the kind merchant to his servants, "and give him a good meal. After that, he can stay and work for the cook as far as he is able."

Now Dick would have been very happy in Mr. Fitzwarren's house, if it hadn't been for the ill-natured cook. She was always shouting and shaking her ladle at him, and she would beat him with a broom or anything else that was handy.

There was another problem, too. Poor Dick had to sleep in a garret full of rats and mice. The place was overrun with them, and he could not sleep at night.

One day, however, a gentleman gave Dick a penny for cleaning his shoes, and Dick used the money to buy a cat. Puss turned out to be a splendid mouser, and Dick had no more trouble with rats and mice.

Soon after this, Mr. Fitzwarren had a ship ready to sail. He liked to give his servants a chance of good fortune too, so he called them all to him and asked what they could send. Most had money, or goods that could be sold in distant countries. But poor Dick had nothing, only his cat. "Send the cat then," said Mr. Fitzwarren.

Dick was very sad to part with his cat. "Now I'll be kept awake all night by the rats and mice," he said.

Everyone laughed at Dick for sending his cat on a voyage — everyone except Mr. Fitzwarren's daughter, Alice, who was a kind girl and gave Dick some money to buy another cat.

Unfortunately, Alice's kindness made the cook jealous, and after this she was even more cruel to Dick. At last he thought he could stand her ill-treatment no longer. He packed up his things and decided to run away.

He left London and walked as far as Holloway, high above the city. There he sat down on a stone, wondering which road he should take. As he sat there, he heard the sound of the bells of Bow Church in the distance. They seemed to say:

"Turn again, Whittington,
Thrice Lord Mayor of London."

"Lord Mayor of London!" he said to himself. "Well, I could put up with anything if I'm to be Lord Mayor one day and ride in a fine coach. I'll go back to Mr. Fitzwarren's house, and I won't run away again."

Meanwhile, Mr. Fitzwarren's ship, with the cat on board, had reached the coast of Africa and was driven by the winds to the shores of a country called Barbary. The people there were most curious to see the sailors and to inspect the fine things that the ship had brought.

The King of the country soon sent for the ship's captain, who gathered all his best and finest goods to take to the palace. There he spread them out in a great room, on rich carpets flowered with gold and silver. The King and Queen sat at the far end of the room, and a number of splendid dishes were brought in for dinner.

But as soon as the food was placed before them, a great army of rats and mice rushed in and ate up everything in an instant.

"The King would give half his treasure to be free of these rats and mice," said one of the servants to the captain.

The captain was very excited when he heard this, for he remembered

Dick Whittington's cat. "Sir," he said to the King, "I have a creature on my ship that will destroy all these rats and mice immediately."

The King was delighted at the news. "If that is true," he said, "I will load your ship with gold and jewels in exchange for this incredible animal."

"Well," said the captain, "I would be very sorry to lose her, for rats and mice might well overrun my ship, but just to oblige your Majesty, I'll fetch her."

He went back to the ship and returned to the palace with the cat. In an instant she had cleared the great hall of almost all the rats and mice, and those that were left ran away in fright.

"But this is wonderful!" said the King.

"Oh, do let me have a look at this creature," said the Queen. The captain presented the cat to her. At first she was a little afraid to touch this strange animal that had attacked the rats and mice so fiercely, but the captain put Puss on her lap where she purred and played gently with the Queen's hand, and then fell asleep.

When the King learned that Puss's kittens would stock the whole country and keep it free from mice, he was delighted. He bought the entire ship's cargo and gave the captain ten times as much for the cat as for all the rest.

The ship then set sail and, after a calm voyage, arrived safely in London. What a story the captain had to tell Mr. Fitzwarren! The kind merchant was amazed to hear about Dick's cat, and immediately sent for the poor boy.

"He must be called Mr. Whittington now," said Mr. Fitzwarren.

Dick was scouring pots for the cook when the servants came to find him. He was very dirty and was reluctant to go with them, fearing that they were only playing a joke on him.

"Please don't make fun of me," he said. "Let me go back to my work."

"Mr. Whittington," said the merchant, when Dick stood before him, "the captain has sold your cat to the King of Barbary and has brought you in return for her more wealth than I possess in the whole world. Long may you live to enjoy these riches!" And he showed Dick the treasure the captain had brought.

Dick didn't know what to say. "I beg you," he told the good merchant, "take whatever you want."

Mr. Fitzwarren refused. "No," he said. "It is yours. I'm sure you'll use it wisely."

Dick asked Mrs. Fitzwarren and his master's daughter, Alice, if they would accept part of the treasure, but they too refused, while congratulating him on his good fortune. Dick was too kind-hearted to keep it all to himself, however, and he gave handsome presents to the captain, the mate, and the servants in the house – even to the bad-tempered cook!

When Dick was dressed in fine clothes he looked as good as any young man in London. He and Alice Fitzwarren fell in love, and, her father giving his consent to the match, they were soon married. The Lord Mayor and all the richest merchants in London came to their wedding.

Dick Whittington and his wife lived happily ever after. Dick became Sheriff of London and three times Lord Mayor, and the King made him Sir Richard.

> "Turn again, Whittington,
> Thrice Lord Mayor of London."

So had said the bells of Bow, and they were right – the poor boy *did* become Lord Mayor of London.

# THE CITY MOUSE
# AND THE
# COUNTRY MOUSE

Æsop

A LETTER for you," said the postman.

"Who can it be from?" said the Country Mouse. She didn't often get letters for she knew very few people outside the little village.

"Open it and see," said the postman. So the Country Mouse tore open the envelope.

"It's from my cousin in the city," she said, her eyes sparkling and her whiskers twitching. "She's coming to visit. How exciting!"

"Dear Cousin," wrote the City Mouse. "It has been a very long time since we saw each other. I think it is time I paid you a visit. I shall arrive on Saturday."

Well, what a scurrying and bustling and polishing there was that week. The Country Mouse cleaned her little nest from top to bottom. "How fresh and tidy it all looks," she said to herself, very pleased with her efforts.

"I'm sure my cousin will like this beautiful place," she thought. "And won't she enjoy all the fresh air after being cooped up in the city for so long!"

Saturday came and all was ready for the visit. The Country Mouse had prepared a special dinner of wheat stalks and roots that she had gathered from the hedgerows.

Early in the afternoon, the Country Mouse heard a carriage draw up. She rushed to the door, and there was her cousin. How smart the City Mouse looked! She wore a fine silk gown trimmed with lace, and her jewels looked real!

"Come in! Welcome!" cried the Country Mouse.

"What a journey!" The City Mouse fanned herself. "I thought I'd never get here. So this is where you live!" And she sniffed.

"I've made dinner," said the Country Mouse. "We'll eat first – you

must be hungry. And afterwards, I'll take you over the fields."

The City Mouse shuddered. "Oh, no thank you. Fields – so muddy and dirty, and you might get lost."

The Country Mouse laughed, and set out the simple meal she had prepared.

She was sorry to see that the City Mouse just picked at her plate. She left most of the delicious wheat stalks and just nibbled at the turnip roots.

As the days went by, the Country Mouse found her cousin very difficult to please. She didn't want to explore the fields: she only yawned when the Country Mouse begged her to listen to the song of the lark. She was quite clearly bored by the chatter of the other mice, who talked about the fields and the seasons and narrow escapes from the gamekeeper and all sorts of things that didn't interest her at all.

One morning she said to the Country Mouse: "You poor thing. I am so sorry for you. But don't worry – I have a splendid plan."

"Sorry? For me?" The Country Mouse was bewildered. "But why?"

"Look at you," said the City Mouse. "You live in this hovel. You eat the poorest and plainest of food. And what a dull life you lead! You never meet anyone interesting. It's time you had a change. Come with me to the city. You have no idea how well we city mice live! We feast on the very best of food and we live in the greatest of comfort. Do come! We can set off this very day!"

The Country Mouse had found her cousin's visit a little trying. The City Mouse didn't seem to enjoy anything. But it was kind of her to suggest a visit to the city. The Country Mouse had never been away from her own village. As the City Mouse went on describing the city – the feasting, the entertainment, the clever and amusing mice who lived there – the Country Mouse thought, "I must see this! It will be a great adventure." So she thanked her cousin and went off to get ready. She packed her best dress and a clean pinafore, and off they went to catch the coach to the city.

It was night when the two mice crept into the great house. "It is safer this way," whispered the City Mouse.

The Country Mouse was very surprised at this. She had not thought there would be any danger in the city. She looked around the great house in amazement at the beautiful silver and glass and the magnificent paintings and rich furnishings.

"Ah, good," said the City Mouse. "They have left us some of the feast."

The Country Mouse wondered who her cousin meant by "they," but she didn't say anything.

"Come along, Cousin," said the City Mouse. "Help yourself. You must be hungry after the journey."

The Country Mouse had never seen such a magnificent spread. There on the splendid table was everything a mouse could wish for – bread and beans, and honey and raisins, and meat, and the most delicious cheese in a basket. "Go on," said the City Mouse. "Eat all you want."

The Country Mouse hardly knew where to begin. But before she had a chance even to nibble a piece of bread, the City Mouse exclaimed, "Shh! Someone's coming! Run as fast as you can! Follow me!" and raced towards a narrow hole in the woodwork. From there, the two mice peered out as a servant girl entered the dining room to clear up the remains of the banquet.

"What is it? Why are we hiding?" asked the Country Mouse in astonishment.

"Shh . . . don't say a word." The City Mouse was trembling in fear.

They waited for a few moments, and then the girl left the room. "Now's our chance!" said the City Mouse. "There are still some crumbs left."

The two mice crept out of their hiding place and began to nibble at the remaining food. But they had hardly started when the door opened again and this time a manservant came in. He carried a tray of glasses which he placed in a cupboard.

Again the two mice scurried for safety and watched him from their hiding place.

"See how comfortable it is!" said the City Mouse to her cousin. "How warm and snug we are in this hole, compared to your draughty little nest . . ."

The Country Mouse didn't say anything. She was so hungry! She had hardly begun to nibble the cheese before they were disturbed. If only she had a few wheat stalks and some roots!

Next day it was no better. It was seldom safe to go out, and the two mice watched, twitching with fear, as the servants carried food to the table, then removed the remains of the feast.

"This won't do," said the Country Mouse. She put her best dress and her pinafore back into her basket.

"Why, what are you doing, cousin?" asked the City Mouse.

"I am going home," said the Country Mouse, very firmly. "I know you have the best of fare here. But you must enjoy it on your own. I'd rather live on plain fare in peace than dine luxuriously in fear. Goodbye, cousin!"

That night the Country Mouse settled back into her own home after a delicious meal of wheat stalks. "Ah," she said to herself. "I did enjoy that." And she went peacefully to sleep.

# GLOSSARY OF DIFFICULT WORDS

*The Wicked Lord Chamberlain and the Kind Animals*

flunkey – a manservant in uniform

*Tiger in the Forest, Anansi in the Web*

gibnut and accouri – wild animals of the forest, prized as delicacies by the Indians of Central America

plantain – a tropical flowering plant with large leaves, very similar to a banana

marmoset – a small South American monkey with a long, hairy tail, clawed fingers and toes, and tufts of hair around the head and ears

capuchin monkey – an agile, intelligent monkey that lives in the forests of South America and has a hood of thick fur on the top of its head

*Rikki-tikki-tavi*

cantonment – a permanent military camp in India, when India was ruled by the British (before 1947)

tailor-bird – a singing bird with a long bill and slender feet, found in India. As described in the story, the tailor-bird takes cotton from the cotton shrub, spins it to a thread with its long bill, and then stitches the edges of leaves together to make a hollow for its nest

draggled – wet and dirty as a result of being dragged along the ground

dust-bath – the action of a small animal or bird when it drives dust into its fur or feathers to dislodge parasites

# ACKNOWLEDGMENTS

The publishers gratefully acknowledge permission to include the following stories:

"The Wicked Lord Chamberlain and the Kind Animals," "Farmer Giles's Goats," "Chanticleer and Pertelotte" and "The Sparrows' Tug-of-War" all retold by Stephen Corrin. Reproduced by kind permission of the author.

"Bertrand and Ratto," "The Grateful Beasts," "The Council Held by the Rats," "The Tomtit and the Bear," "The Cat and the Fox," "The Musicians of Bremen," "Brer Rabbit's Good Children," "Dick Whittington and His Cat," and "The City Mouse and the Country Mouse," all retold by Anne Forsyth. Copyright © 1991 by Anne Forsyth.

"Tiger in the Forest, Anansi in the Web" retold by Philip Sherlock. Copyright © 1966 by Philip Sherlock. Reprinted from *West Indian Folk-tales* (1966) by permission of Oxford University Press.

"The Wolf and the Seven Little Kids," "The Three Goats Called Hurricane" and "The Dog and the Wolf," retold by Catherine Taylor. Copyright © 1991 by Catherine Taylor.

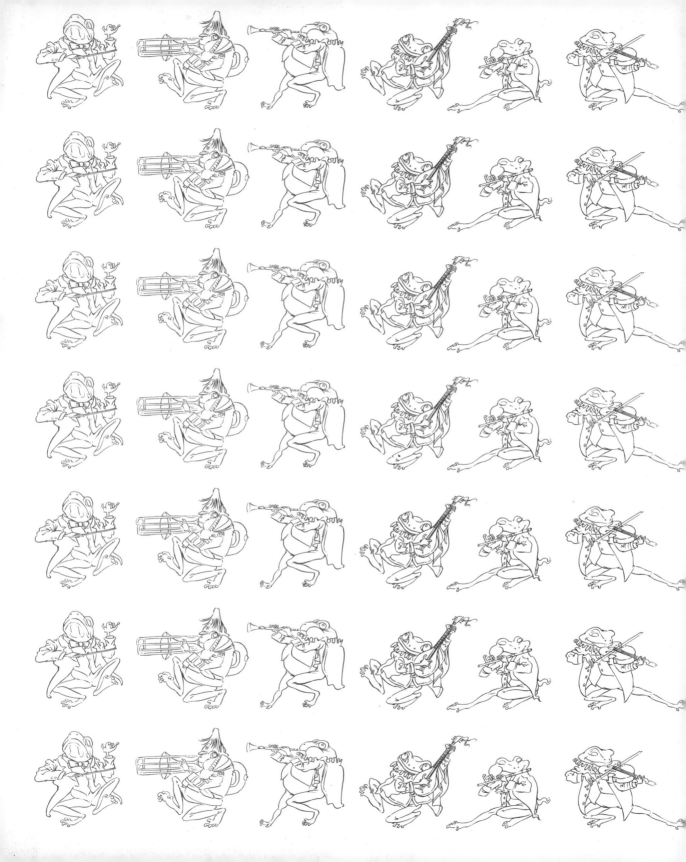